ROWING

HOME

Nathan Clark Ticknor

Acknowledgements

First I would like to thank Julia Petrakis for her edits, advice, and encouragement- without her this edition would not exist. Also I would like to thank my family for all their love and support, not only in this endeavor but throughout my life. A special thanks to my grandmother, Shirley, for her special encouragement of my writing, her interest in my stories, and pushing me to do more than just write them. On a trip to Maine with my grandfather, William, the idea for this novel was planted in my soul. I would like to thank him for that amazing trip and for his work editing and advising early on in the process. To my parents, Bill and Cheryl, thank you for your endless support and providing me with the life experiences including travel, which set a stirring in my soul from a young age. My brother, Andrew, and my sister, Michelle, I love you both so much and thank you for your friendship and love, but also for reading my works and listening to my endless chatter about family history. Without my ancestors paving the way and providing me with this opportunity none of this would be possible. I would like to add a special mention to my forefather, William Davis Ticknor, who started the family in the literary tradition back in 1832 when he founded the publishing house which would come to be known as Ticknor and Fields.

Rowing Home
Second Edition

ISBN 978-1-257-86126-2

For

S.A.T & W.D.T. III

From Tirra Lirra, Tiny Bill 'til Now

ONE

My gut wrenched as I placed the phone back on the holder on my desk. Stunned I could do nothing but stare out my office window at the park where there were always children playing on the junglegym. Typically, there would be parents making small talk as they pushed their young children on the swings, kids running around in circles chasing each other, or even a poor little girl crying for her brother to stop spinning her around and around in the tire swing. But today it was empty and rain just formed puddles in the areas beaten down from the paths of the children.

Suddenly so many questions flooded my mind: this can't be right, why him, how did it happen, why did it happen, am I dreaming? I shook my head as if the gesture could rid my mind of the nagging questions. Luckily I had no more appointments for the rest of the day, so when I finally regained enough composure, I told my secretary I would be leaving and to reschedule my appointments for the next several days.

As I walked out of the office, I put my coat on and pulled the collar up around my neck in an attempt to stay as dry as possible. I held my breath, took a step and jogged out through the steady rain to the parking lot. When I got to my car, I pulled open the door and hastily jumped into the comfort of its dry interior. I took a deep breath, put my key in the ignition and grabbed the wheel. I would drive to Maine, returning to the town in which I had spent the better part of my life, the place in which my life was turned around.

I drove home slowly, not noticing anything along the way. Even the radio fell silent with the sound of the rain landing on the car's roof and the wipers' occasional interruption to clear the windshield. I pulled into my driveway and had one of those moments when you try to think back on a trip, but you can't remember any of the details. I sat in my car watching the garage door slowly lift, feeling as though I could relate to the garage, this great weight that it was required to carry. Then I wondered if that thought would make sense to anyone but me. Before I let my mind get in too much of a mess, I pulled into the garage and got out.

My little house in suburban Chicago had never seemed so empty. It's funny how when someone you knew and loved dies, no matter how far away they are at the time or how long it has been since you last saw them, their absence weighs heavily and makes places they've never even been seem all the emptier for their no longer being in the world. I reached up and took a glass from the cupboard, filling it with water and then made my way to the couch in the family room where I collapsed. Hemingway, the mutt I rescued from the pound a couple of years ago, came running downstairs and with his dog-like sense knew that something was wrong and fit his body perfectly beside mine, as if to say, "I'm here for you." I don't know if it was Hemingway's presence or I was finally ready but I allowed myself to say it, "He's gone, Ben is dead, Benjamin Stockbridge is finally in heaven."

The last phrase brought a slight peace with it. It was the truth. I had no doubt that at that very moment, Ben was in the middle of a glorious reunion in heaven, one he had been looking forward to for a long time, and one that gave me solace. I started scratching Hemingway's head, which he had affectionately placed on my chest; his heavy panting seemed to calm me with its steady rhythm. I had known this day would eventually come, but I had pictured it at least 30 years from now; I hadn't even known if I would still be around.

But I guess this was no big surprise; it kind of fit in place with the rest of Ben's life. As I sat there reflecting on his life and the times we had together, I regretted how long it had been since I had last seen him. Searching through my mind, I realized it had been seven years since our paths last crossed. As so often happens when a death occurs, I began to wish I had treasured him more while he was alive. I looked down at Hemingway still lying peacefully next to me.

"What am I going to do with you?" The question hadn't yet crossed my mind; I knew I couldn't leave him at my house while I was gone. My mom's house was definitely not an option; the poor lady could hardly manage herself day to day. Hemingway would do her in. I could call my Grandmother, and ask her if it would be OK for me to bring him. Hemingway would love Maine. "How would you like a trip to the Maine Coast?" Hemingway must've sensed the meaning of my words because he jumped off the couch, unintentionally digging his claws into my stomach; he stood eagerly waiting for me, as he often would before we would go for walks. I stood up and looked through the sliding glass doors at the rain, which was coming down even stronger now. "Not today buddy, but soon, soon enough," I tried to console him.

Stretching I walked to the stairs and decided to pack my bags so I could leave first thing in the morning. As I sorted through my closet and pulled things from my drawers, holding my cell phone between my shoulder and ear, I called my Grandmother to make sure it would be alright if Hemingway came along. The phone rang seven times before Grandma finally answered her old dial phone. I heard her clear her throat twice before her sweet voice broke through, "Hello?" "Gran, it's me Sam again," she was the one on the other end of the call I had received in my office earlier which set all this in motion. "Sweet Sam, how are you doing with things?"

We made small talk for awhile as I continued haphazardly packing my bags. She said she'd be thrilled if Hemingway came, and I realized I knew she wouldn't care. I could've asked if she would mind if I brought an axe murderer, she still would've said she'd be thrilled. That's just how Gran is. I told her I was planning to leave around six in the morning so if there weren't any problems I should get in around midnight. The thought of the drive made me exhausted; it would be refreshing though since I hadn't been that way in years and it would give me time to think and remember the great times with Ben. My emotions and thoughts were making me feel physically spent. I decided to just go up and lie in bed, hoping to fall asleep and wake up early to get a good head start on my trip. It was only five in the afternoon but I didn't care. I closed the blinds, put on my shorts and got in my bed with Hemingway at my feet.

I am lost in a forest. The red and white pines rise so high I can't see the sky. The ground is covered with snow and my shoes are soaked. Every step I take, icy water squishes through my toes. The cold harsh wind bites at my face and I tuck my nose under my arm to protect it and warm it but there is ice frozen on the sleeve that scratches my nose and makes the cold even worse. I can hardly see three feet in front of me. I am more scared than I've been in years, and I am utterly lost. Then I hear my name, "Sam, where are you?" I open my mouth to scream for help. With everything in me I try to yell, but no sound comes out. I sit there until all my energy is spent trying to scream. Finally I give up and lying my shaking body on the snow, I am content to just lie there and die. Then I feel the warmth of a hand on my arm and before I know it, I am looking through the swirling snow at Ben. There with his big beard again, smiling down at me. He helps me to my feet and guides me through the snowbound pine forest to a clearing where the sun shines in the distance and a dirt path emerges and travels through fields of green grass. I immediately run to the path and then realize Ben is no longer beside me. I turn and see his face being swallowed by darkness in the forest; the cold engulfs him as he slowly fades out of view. He never grimaces in pain or changes his expression. And then he is completely gone.

I woke up soaked in sweat and thirsty. Hemingway was gone and the room was dark. I checked my watch; it was nine, I had been asleep for four hours. I got up and poured a glass of cold water. The thought of leaving for Maine right then crossed my mind, but I decided a few more hours of sleep would do me good. I got back in bed and lay there trying to fall back asleep, wondering how I would find the little town of Camden, if anything had changed. I had so many memories of that place, some of the best and worst times of my life. The most trying times of my life were spent there; I looked forward to returning and regretted that it took Ben's death to take me back. I bore Camden no ill will; it was just that life had been busy and it was never at the top of my priorities to return. It was always something I would do the next year. Truth be told, I had never been to Camden until I was 16, but that was an area and time in my life I didn't have the energy to look back on tonight. When I finally fell back asleep, I was picturing what meal Gran would have ready for me. I pictured her busy at work, making a special blueberry cobbler, my old favorite and running to the grocery to buy some vanilla ice-cream for me to have with it.

The night is dark, the clouds choke the light of the stars out of sight and the moon is nowhere to be found. I'm in a skiff without any oars and no sails to get my way back to shore. There is a storm beginning to brew and the waves crash over the side of the boat and soak me with every punch from the sea. I'm trying to get my bearings, to figure out where I am, the salt stings my eyes and I can spot no land anywhere around me. Lost at sea with no way to power my boat and no way to guide me to safety, I feel like a child lost in a mall with no sight of his parent, vulnerable and helpless. Then something breaks the darkness; it's a large spotlight, skimming the surface of the sea, I hear the humming of an outboard motor from the same direction and then I see Ben standing in the bow of the boat, searching intently with his eyes. When they make contact with mine, he immediately re-directs his boat and comes to pick me up. I say nothing and neither does Ben, he just motors back to the dock. The dock looks different than I remember; it is lighted all the way down and a warm inn is at the end with smoke gently rising from the chimney, bringing the smell of a warm meal. I step out of the boat and begin walking towards the inn. Looking back halfway down the dock, I expect to see Ben tying up the boat and then coming to join me for the meal, but I just catch him looking over his shoulder as his boat disappears in the dark of the night sea. I hear no motor, just his boat drifting out to sea.

Waking up, I realized I had dreamt more in this one night than I remembered dreaming in years. Strange dreams, I thought. Sitting on the edge of my bed, I called for Hemingway and he came bounding into my room. "Get your things ready, Hemi; we're heading to Maine." I laughed to myself at the thought of telling my dog to get his things ready. After deciding not to shave, an old habit I had when I would go to Maine, I hopped in the shower and then started brewing some coffee as I poured my cereal. I checked my watch; it was three in the morning. I put Hemingway in the backyard while I loaded the car with my suitcase and garment bag. Back inside, I filled my thermos to the top with hot coffee, added my cream, no sugar, called Hemingway and got in the car. As I drove out of town and got on the highway, I drifted back in my mind to the first time I had left the Chicago area to move to Maine.

Back when I was 16 years old, I was a much different person than I am now. I was a teenager full of anger: Anyone who had tried to be my friend, I had pushed away and even made an effort to hurt. I prided myself on my vile language and didn't care what company I was in when the words spewed from my mouth. Whenever I got a chance, I would instigate a fight, be it with a classmate, a stranger, or even a teacher.

A series of events in my childhood had led to the lost, hopeless kid that I was. I had been expelled from school and forced to talk to a school psychiatrist, spilling some secrets from my past for the first time. As soon as I did, I regretted having told him. I had hoped that if I told him these things he would be on my side and help me get out of the trouble I was in. Come to find out, though, he took that information and used it against my mom and the man that at the time I termed, "the bastard of a stepdad."

My grandparents, Loring and Judith Slade, had offered to let me live with them in Maine. I had never been to Maine, but they had made several trips to Chicago to visit me. They weren't too bad; I decided I liked the prospect of Maine over the thought of having to have foster parents, so I agreed. My grandparents both drove from Camden, Maine to Chicago to pick me up.

I remember that day vividly. I knew it was goodbye to my mom and my stepdad, so I thought I would leave them with a stinger. "Bye, Mom, hope you survive this asshole," I said, and pointing at my step-dad, "I hope you go to hell." With that, I walked out of the house and sat with my single bag on the curb. I could hear my mom crying on the inside and my stepdad shouting something I couldn't make out. My grandparents drove up in grandpa's old Chevy truck. Gran got out and gave me the first hug I had received in years, one I didn't reciprocate. My grandpa, whom I called Pops, shook my hand and said he was glad I was going to live with them and said Maine could teach me a lot, in response to which I just let out a sarcastic laugh. They asked where my mom was; I lied and said she was out. No doubt they knew I was lying, what with the noises coming from the house. We all three loaded up in the truck and drove out of town on the same route I was now retracing back to Camden, Maine.

The drive today was uneventful. Being so early, the streets were empty and with Hemingway to keep me company, I listened to the radio. I would sing along, sip my coffee and talk aloud to Hemingway who held his nose to the barely cracked window, occasionally trying to fit his head through or widen the crack.

Those thoughts of my first drive to Maine hadn't crossed my mind in years; those were the days before Ben had entered in my life. My grandparents were very considerate on that trip. The psychiatrist had told my grandparents the story I had told him, so they knew not to ask any details. If they had, I probably would have jumped out of the truck no matter where we were. When they did talk, they always mentioned how much I would like Maine and how excited they were that I was going to be a daily part of their lives. I laughed to myself, knowing I would probably cause them a lot of pain, because I had no intention of changing.

I have never admitted it to anyone, but I was fascinated by everything I saw on that drive. I had never been outside of Chicago in my life and driving through the Midwest and into New England offered me a glimpse of a world I had never known. I had seen it in books and movies, but for the first time in my life, I was experiencing it for myself. We stopped halfway and stayed at a little hotel. We were all pretty exhausted, but the next day they had me up bright and early, and we were on our way again. I remember the closer we got to Maine, the more I enjoyed the scenery. It seemed as though I was leaving my old life behind and going into some story-book place. It was refreshing to know that no one knew me in Camden—or anywhere in Maine, for that matter. As soon as we crossed the border, we stopped and got sub sandwiches and I really enjoyed myself.

13

After lunch, Loring, Judith and I hopped back into the truck and started the last leg of the drive. As we drove into Maine on State Route 1, I caught my first glimpses of Penobscot Bay, and for the first time in my life, something in nature made me feel warm and accepted. I remember being very fond of that feeling, and at that time I decided I would chase that feeling and do anything to keep it. During the short trip through town, my grandparents explaining each and every little store and shop to me, my eyes the whole time kept their constant gaze on the bay.

My grandparents' place was just north of town on a small piece of land surrounded on two sides by the water with a small rocky peninsula or "point" that jutted out into the bay. Enormous trees rose throughout the property and Pops explained that they were red and white pines. As I got out of the truck, I stepped onto a blanket of red pine needles. I looked over at Pops and his eyes were closed and his arms were up with his hands meeting behind his head as he took a long slow deep breath. "There's nothing in the world like Maine air, Sam."

Their house was simple, a small Cape Cod. It had been, at one point, sky blue with white trim, but now more of the wood beneath the paint shown through than actual paint. The raggedy look of the house immediately made me fond of it. I felt like it could relate to me. It seemed to have been through lots of wear and tear, and I felt relaxed there in its presence. There was a porch that wrapped all the way around the house, which looked as though it had been built some years after the house itself. Later I would learn it had been my Gran's lifelong dream to have a wraparound porch and on one of their wedding anniversaries, Pops had started building her one. The door was in the middle of the house and there was a window on either side of it. The upstairs had two windows and there was a chimney of rugged old bricks on the right side of the house.

The house was in a clearing of pines and there was a small stone path from the porch to the driveway. I helped my grandpa carry the bags in and they showed me the house. As soon as you walked in, there was the small living room with a shabby green couch, an aged lamp and elegant rocking chair opposite the couch. In all the free spaces along the wall were dark-wood bookcases, which rose to about chest height. They were filled on every single shelf with old, weathered, dusty books. Along the walls, were old, framed, black-and-white photographs of my grandparents when they were younger. On a small corner table was a framed picture of me when I was ten years old. I hated that picture, and I immediately decided my first mission would be to get rid of it.

The air was musty and old; a scent I would grow to appreciate but had not yet acquired a taste for. Standing in the doorway there was a door directly to the left when you walked in, which led to Gran's and Pop's bedroom. Looking to the right past the fireplace, which was the half-way point in the family room, was the dining area, consisting of a small round wooden table, with three chairs, two of them old, and one which seemed to be new, not even stained yet. Walking through the dining area led to the kitchen, which had a door leading to the rear porch and right past the kitchen was a spiral staircase which matched the rest of the house in wear and tear. It led to the upstairs bedroom, my bedroom, which took up the whole upper level. Past the bottom of the stairs was the one bathroom, which we all shared, and had a door which led to my grandparents' room.

My bedroom was by far the biggest room in the house. The walls were newly painted fresh white and the dark-wood floor stood out in stark contrast. Light was pouring in from the four windows, which protruded from the walls and ceiling, giving the house the Cape-Cod look. There was an empty closet and a bed with the most inviting quilt of red, white and blue I had ever seen. Next to the bed was a nightstand

15

with a small clock on it and on the wall across from the bed was a bookshelf. It too was filled to the top with all kinds of books, all dusty, whose titles could barely be made out from the spines, some of which were not so old, but looked almost to have been old library books. There was a single picture in the whole room, a painted picture of an old tall sailing ship being tossed about in a storm, with waves crashing all around it. It was framed with a wood frame, whose corners looked as though it had been years since they fit together as they were intended. I threw my suitcases on the bed and laughed to myself at the situation I was now in, quite a long way from my house in Chicago.

I heard Pops yell up the stairs that whenever I felt comfortable he wanted to take me around to see the property. I lay on the bed staring at the ceiling for awhile, feeling quite overwhelmed and not knowing exactly what to make of everything. It almost seemed as though I was dreaming a very peaceful, relaxing dream. My problems seemed far away for the moment, but I knew they were secretly just lurking moments away and some small event or thought could trigger a tempest of emotions sending me on a meltdown. That thought scared me and I no longer wanted to be alone so I ran down to Pops.

He and Gran were sitting down at the table and enjoying a steaming cup of tea, what I would soon learn was a common practice of theirs. I sat down with them and looked out the rear window. There were two rocking chairs on the porch and several trees were the only objects obscuring the view of the shoreline of the bay not more than twenty yards from the house. Slightly to the right a small pebble path led from the porch to a house that was painted in the same fashion as the one we were in and had aged to the same degree. I would learn it was the boathouse, and outside in front of it was a ramp and a slip out into the bay.

When Pops had finished his tea, he looked up at me with his old blue eyes and offered a smile. "Well, we'll be back, Dear," he said as he leaned over and kissed Gran. I followed him out of through the back door and he walked out to the point, out on to the rocks and I matched him step for step until we were there. It was a view unlike any I had ever seen before; to my left the rocky shore was lined with large pines reaching high into the sky. Intermixed among the pines were white birches, stretching their branched arms out over the water, while small waves lapped against the stones. To the right, some birds were diving not far off in the surf and I could see in the distance the town of Camden and Camden Harbor. Squinting my eyes, I could see there were many boats, of different sizes, shapes, and colors, all so new to me. I loved the boats. They filled me with anticipation of some wonderful adventures.

Above the city I could see a white steeple poking into the sky above the other buildings. For the first time, without thinking about it, I closed my eyes, took a deep breath and smiled. As soon as I realized what I was doing I opened my eyes, hoping Pops hadn't seen it. He put his arm on my shoulder, which made me incredibly uncomfortable, and I jerked away. "I'm sorry Sam, I know you've been through a lot and life has been tough. I promise, Gran and I will do everything in our power to give you a better life here. I'm sorry you had to go through what you went through."

As he spoke these words my heart got carried away and was beating uncontrollably, my jaw locked and the joy of the scenery was gone. I hated him for even mentioning the past and I stormed away into the house, not looking over at Gran, still sitting at the table when I walked in. I went straight to my bedroom. That is when I went to the bookshelf in my room for the first time. Blindly reaching, I pulled out one of the dusty old books. I blew on it, and realized most of the dust was there to stay. I gazed down at the small book in my hand, no words

17

on the front, just an elaborate golden design centered on the faded blue cover; I turned the book in my hand looking for a title. There it was on the spine. The years had taken their toll on this book. I struggled to make out the words, *The Seaside and the Fireside,* and just below the title, "Longfellow." The name sounded familiar, but I couldn't match it to anything.

To my knowledge I had never once finished a book. I had been assigned a great many in school, but it was a badge of pride that I never read them. After flipping through several blank pages at the front of the book, I finally came to the title page and the author's name, Henry Wadsworth Longfellow. Flipping to the next page, I saw the date 1849. That is when it struck me that it was probably the oldest thing I had ever held. Staring at the table of contents, I decided to try an entry on page 32, "The Secret of the Sea." I figured since my new home was on the sea it would be a good thing to know its secret. So I began to read from the browned, spotted pages.

Not quite understanding all I was reading or grasping the meaning of the words, my frustration grew. There was no secret, I was able to comprehend; as I continued to read through, I neared the end. I now know the words by heart.

"Wouldst thou,"--so the helmsman answered,
  "Learn the secret of the sea?
Only those who brave its dangers
  Comprehend its mystery!"

In each sail that skims the horizon,
  In each landward-blowing breeze,
I behold that stately galley,
  Hear those mournful melodies;

Till my soul is full of longing
   For the secret of the sea,
And the heart of the great ocean
   Sends a thrilling pulse through me.

I lay down on my bed with the book on my chest, and thought over the phrase, "… the secret of the sea…" I wanted to understand and to grasp it all, but I wasn't quite there. As I lay there deep in thought, I slowly drifted to sleep.

Suddenly I was startled back into the present with a wet tongue right in my ear. "Hemingway, come on, man." He looked up at me with his brown-sugar colored eyes, and I realized in my nostalgia thinking back on my first trip to Maine, I had forgotten to take care of Hemingway and his bladder. For the next several miles, I was scanning the horizon for rest area signs. When you are not looking for a rest area they seem to occur about every five miles, but when you are on a frantic search for one, they decide to make an appearance every 116 miles or so. Such was the case and the longer I drove without stopping the more worried I became that I would spend a lot of time cleaning dog urine from my car. Not a pleasant task. But finally the rest area came like a savior. Hemingway and I both eager for a break, enjoyed a quick half hour stop there with a packed lunch which consisted of peanut butter and jelly for myself and a nice bowl of dog food for Hemingway. I sat on the edge of a splintery picnic table and threw a tennis ball for him to retrieve, which he did eagerly. Mini vans full of frantic families pulled up and screaming children ran to the rest area. I enjoyed the warmth of the sun on my face. Briefly I wished I could close my eyes and then open them to find myself standing on Gran's front porch, but then I realized this drive was something I needed and it provided a lot of time to think. Sitting there, I realized I hadn't had time off from work in as long as I could remember.

The calm summer day was suddenly broken by the roaring of a dying, if not already dead, muffler. Hemingway started barking and I looked up to see an old beat up car, which looked as though it had been lucky to start. A young man about twenty years old got out, his eyes red as if he had done a great deal of crying and there was a certain essence of sorrow about him. I wondered what was his story? What great secret or tragedy he was dealing with? Who was helping him through? To me, the greatest tragedy in life was when people had to carry great sorrow and pain, alone, in silence -- because I had lived that pain and I knew I could relate. But I knew that if I was to get to Maine at a decent time I needed to get back on the road. I had already lingered too long. After throwing away the trash from lunch and collecting Hemingway's bowls, we loaded back in the car and continued on our journey.

We were somewhere in mid-state New York and the late sun of summer had begun to fall behind the tall trees, creating a brief array of colors before the darkness of night consumed the last minutes of light and the stars shone through and the crescent moon appeared. I loved the sky. Looking up through the window of my sunroof, I felt as if I saw more stars than I did in an average week back in Chicago. Ever since that first experience standing at my grandparent's house, 16 years ago, nature seemed to make me thankful, to give me peace and to permit me to believe in something bigger. Looking up at the night sky was one of those moments. Hemingway was now sleeping; his body sprawled out on the entire back seat, his tongue hanging, dripping saliva all over. I drove on into the night, finding myself in great company with Hemingway sleeping in the back, the stars shining overhead, the trees keeping watch on the sides and the radio singing to keep me up.

Finally after an exhausting day of driving, I neared Camden. The roadside was lined with the ever-familiar pines and birches, which now were shadows in the night. I drove through the town, the only car on the deserted night road. Passing the city, I headed to the rocky point where Gran still lived after all these years. The only light to be seen as I turned to the winding driveway was the light of my headlights illuminating the path before me. Hemingway was up now, sitting in the front seat, eagerly anticipating the end of the drive. Through the trees ahead I could make out the lights of the house I was so fond of. As I pulled my car to a stop, Gran came from the house.

The years had taken their toll on her and the past seven years since Pops had died, she seemed to have accelerated even more down the path of aging we all fight so hard to avoid. The years may have worn heavily on her body, but her joy was as evident as it had been her entire life. As I got out of the car, Hemingway came running out behind me. He immediately began sniffing the premises and I received a wonderful hug from Gran. Through the years, mostly in these later years as her balance and mobility began to decline, her hugs became a way for her to steady herself and I could feel her wrapping her arms about me with total reliance. After saying our hellos, I grabbed the bags from the car and took them to my old room.

Gran and I sat down to a cup of hot tea together while I kept an eye on Hemingway's eagerly wagging tail to make sure it didn't knock over anything in the house. The house looked much like it did in all of my memories. Just more pictures. There seemed to be a picture of Pops everywhere. Framed on the wall was my favorite one, the one of us together after my graduation from college, the pride and joy in his eyes always made me feel so special. I could tell she missed Pops a lot. They had a relationship that was something special, something that seemed rare. We sat there talking about my drive, how life had been since we

21

had seen each other last. Then I finally asked it, I don't know why I waited to ask but it just didn't make sense to me.

"So nobody knew Ben was sick, I mean, how could you just go from being that healthy to that sick and nobody notice?" "Well, apparently when he found out he was sick and how severe it was, he didn't want anyone to feel sorry for him or treat him any differently. He just wanted to keep living life the way it was until it was his time, and that is exactly what he did. Now, some of us noticed he was losing a lot of weight and he seemed to have such tiredness about him, but he would either say he had the flu or was just busy, with that great smile of his."

As I sat there, I turned the mug on the table, looking down at the tea swirling within as I thought about things. Gran stood up and walked over, giving me a kiss on my cheek and then making her way to her room for the night. I walked out through the back door and took a step off the porch; the familiar feeling of the needles smashing beneath my feet was a welcome memory. I walked out to the point I had loved so much as a teenager, and carefully made my way out to the furthest rock -- so little about the point had changed. Looking back, I could see the dim light of the house and the dark silhouettes of the surrounding trees. Turning out to sea, I could see the moon's soft reflection on the peak of every wave, slowly making its weary way toward the shore. The stars were just as bright and bold as they had been many nights before and I closed my eyes and could hear the crashing of the waves against the stony shore. This was home. Just like the lines of the poem, I had read 16 years ago, I could feel the excitement and desire to be at sea run through my body and as I stood there, I repeated those lines aloud with the stars as my audience.

"Till my soul is full of longing
  For the secret of the sea,
And the heart of the great ocean
  Sends a thrilling pulse through me."

Then I closed my eyes, took a long slow deep breath, and exhaled with a smile on my face.

TWO

The early morning sun shone brightly through the window and warmed my face. The urge to get out of bed had yet to hit me and I decided to lie there, just thinking. As my thoughts wandered through a thousand memories, slowly they all grew older and older until I was thinking back to the first summer I spent in Maine.

Up to that point in my life, I had been a night owl, staying up often until right before sunrise and then sleeping until two or three in the afternoon. But that was one of the first things to change in those early days. Pops and Gran were definitely early to bed and early to rise. Those first nights before I really knew the house and the property, I would ache for something to do and would never find it. No TV, without friends, I would just lie there and think, and that would torment me. Finally, after a couple of nights I broke down and pulled another book off the old shelf, this one dark green with a title in what must have once been brilliant gold, but was now more of a dull gold. *The Maine Woods*. This particular volume was written by Henry David Thoreau, and for lack of better options, I began to read it. At first I told myself this was just to help me fall asleep at night -- and that it did -- but sometimes something deep inside me would think I was actually enjoying reading this book, but I would quickly suppress those feelings.

I now realize that during this point in my life, even though back in Chicago I had been cold, hostile and even cruel to almost everyone, I treated Pops and Gran better. Now I'm not saying I treated them well. I would often have an outbreak of rage and storm off, or say something I knew would cut them deeply just because they seemed so happy, but these events occurred far less frequently than the daily occurrences that had previously become my habit.

I developed a routine of waking up around eight in the morning, about two hours after Pops and Gran, and I would sit down to breakfast with the two of them. Breakfast almost always was scrambled eggs, toast, bacon and coffee, and the love of coffee I developed that summer has remained with me through all the years since. During these breakfast times, I would mostly sit silent, and Pops and Gran would mostly do the same, except for the occasional bit of information or gossip they had heard or read in the paper and felt the urge to pass on. I never let it show, but my favorites of those morning meals were the ones in which we were engaged in constant conversation. Now, these were extremely rare and every time they occurred, as much as I loved them, I couldn't let Pops and Gran think I did, so I would act annoyed or roll my eyes but deep inside I was so happy.

The first day that summer, breakfast consisted only of the sound of silverware clicking against our plates, after which Pops took me out to the point. We walked north along the coast and the border of the property and past the boat house. We had walked about a hundred yards when he cut left, pointing to a turn on the path we were walking on. I hadn't even noticed we were walking along a path. It wasn't really a path but more just needles and dirt that had been worn down by thousands of steps along it, mostly Pops' steps. The path was perfectly straight for about 25 yards until we ran into a small creek where we turned and walked along the creek bank. The peaceful trickling of the water against the moss-covered rocks and the crunch of the needles beneath the soles of our shoes were the only sounds we heard.

The creek led out to the road, close to the driveway, at which point it went under the road. I hadn't even noticed it the night before when we came in. There, we took another left and walking about eight feet from the road, we continued on Pops' trail until we reached the coast. One final left and we walked along to the point where we had started. The property was a nice size and I figured it would help me hide when I didn't want to be around Pops and Gran.

Once we were back at the point, Pops cleared his throat. "That's the property, enjoy it, it's really a marvelous place, Sam. I want to show you the boat house. Are you up for that?"

"Yeah, sure, sounds good."

Of all places on the property, the boathouse grabbed my attention the most. I loved the idea that I would be able to go out on the water by myself with just the boat and be so far from people and everything. I had visions of my rowing out to the bay in the morning and not coming back until evening and not once having to see another person the entire day. It didn't matter to me at the time that I had never before even been in a boat or known anything about the sea. Luckily, when I was younger, my mom had enrolled me in swimming lessons at the YMCA, and I had always loved the water.

Well, Pops and I walked over to the boat house and he got a ring of keys out of his pocket and flipped through until he came to the one he was looking for, unhooked the door, and rolled it open. Immediately, I was in love. My eyes fell on a forest green rowboat. The slabs of wood making up the sides shone in the morning light. The bow and stern both came to a point and there appeared to be slabs across in three places in the boat for people to sit. The trim was white, which stood out beautifully in contrast to the deep green of the sides and interior and on the bow, in white, the name was written: *Santiago*.

"Named it after the old man from *The Old Man and the Sea*. Have you ever read that book?" asked Pops.

"No, never even heard of it."

"Earnest Hemingway, wonderful book. We have it somewhere. I think you'd really like Santiago, a brave old man," he said with a laugh.

I didn't really give any thought to it, just responded with a nod, more eager to just learn how to take the boat out than to hear about the dumb story behind its name. As my eyes scanned the old wooden boat house, I noticed on each side of *Santiago* were old wooden kayaks. On the right side was a pile of wooden oars leaning against the corner of the building. There were lots of different kinds of oars, some with paddles on each side for the kayaks and large ones for the rowboat. Old hooks were scattered along the walls, some with rope hanging haphazardly around them. On the left side of the building was a mass of tackle boxes and fishing poles, as well as nets, lures and an old tin bucket. There was a certain smell to the old boat house, an old musty smell, but I grew quite fond of it.

I was eager to go out in the *Santiago*, but Pops hadn't offered yet. I was doing everything I could think of to show my interest in going out in the rowboat, from staring at the boat, at Pops and at the water. When he would talk, I would just stare at the boat, but he seemed to not pick up on any hints. Finally, I even broke down to the point of desperation and made conversation, asking about the darned rowboat.

"So, when did you buy the rowboat?"

"Buy?" Pops questioned with a laugh, "I made it about fifteen years ago. It really was a fun project."

"You made it?"

Pops just smiled and gave a nod. I was still waiting for him to then say, "Want to go out in it?" but those words never came. To my dismay, the only mention of going out in it was when he said maybe one day I'd be able to row and take it out myself. I wanted to scream, why not today! But I bit my tongue and acted annoyed.

I was short with him for the rest of the day which consisted of hearing about the history of Camden and when he and Gran first moved to the property after they had been married for three years. That was the extent to which I listened to him. He spoke a lot more, but I listened a lot less. When I finally wanted to get out of the house and away from Pops and Gran, I excused myself and walked out to the point. Carefully watching my steps I walked out to the furthest rock, which was a massive stone and I sat there pondering the day. My emotions were a wreck. I was mad that I wasn't able to go out in the boat, but at the same time I was mad at myself for getting so upset at Pops and taking those frustrations out on him and Gran when they really did do so much for me. As I sat there late in the afternoon, it was a beautiful time of day, right before sunset when the world seemed to light up in one last show before the coming night.

As I sat admiring the diving birds and choppy waves coming up and occasionally splashing my legs, I noticed a small boat coming in, away on the horizon. I watched as the boat slowly grew larger as it neared. The vessel seemed to be much like the *Santiago* and there was a single occupant on board, rowing gracefully closer. I could see him look ever so often over his shoulder to check his course towards Camden Harbor. I wondered how long he had been out at sea, and I longed to be him. The only thing I knew was that he had been out to sea and away from the world and that's the only thing I wanted for myself. I watched the oars, which seemed to barely break the surface of the water, and the boat, which gracefully made its way through the chopping surf.

As it neared, I noticed the rower had on an old worn-out flannel shirt and a faded blue Red Sox hat. His strong back seemed to have been forged by hours of rowing out on the waves. As he turned once again, I noticed a large curly beard, which seemed to be brown with almost a red tint to it. Embarrassed that I had just been sitting there, staring at him for who knows how long, I quickly looked away as he nodded his head as if to say "Hi." I thought about quickly running away, but that seemed even creepier, so I just pretended to stare off at the birds flying in the distance.

I sat there wondering who that man was, how he had gotten to be so free. I laughed because he was exactly what I had pictured someone would be who had spent their whole life in Maine. Little did I know then, but that stranger would one day become my best friend. I stole a couple more glances as he rowed farther past the point towards the harbor in the distance. I was startled back to reality by Gran's voice, "Sweet Benjamin, that is the nicest man you could ever meet, but I swear he must carry some pain around with him. He'd give you the shirt off his back in a snowstorm and smile, but his eyes would never cease to be distant. I cannot figure him out." I had no idea what she was talking about. I repeated his name under my breath so Gran couldn't hear me and determined I would learn as much about him as possible, in hopes that I could have what I perceived him to have. The sun had finally set completely and I followed Gran into the house for the evening meal.

It was that same summer that I fell in love. Now, you must understand it wasn't with a person I fell in love but with a wonderful dish known as New England clam chowder. Gran was an expert at making it, and I was hooked by my first taste of that warm, creamy delight. Whenever I asked for it and commented on how much I loved it, Pops and Gran would just laugh and say it is in my blood to love it. Well, it just so happened that night for dinner we were having clam chowder and toasted English muffin bread with the butter melted perfectly on top. Now I'm not sure if it was the longing for the sea, the delight of the clam chowder or the satisfaction with the English muffin bread but I finally began a conversation with my grandparents.

"So who was that Ben guy?"

"What Ben guy?" responded Pops, while Gran hurried to finish chewing her last bite in order to answer my question.

"His name is Benjamin Stockbridge," she finally responded before being interrupted by Pops.

"Oh, that Ben guy."

"He lives just outside the city," she continued. "He bought the house several years ago. Interesting fellow, but sweet as can be. Never mentions where he was before he came here. Anytime anyone asks, he just says he's had some hard times. Boy, can you tell! He's cheerful and always has a smile, but his eyes, oh, those poor eyes are full of a deep sadness, Lord bless his soul."

"He's a great woodsman, kinda works as a handyman and sells fish he catches to make a living. Real interesting fellow. You'll probably meet him at church on Sunday," Pops concluded.

My initial thought was, "Shit! I have to go to church," but then I realized maybe I would get to meet Ben. In my thought process, if I met Ben then maybe he could teach me how to go out to sea, and then finally I could take *Santiago* out and escape the world and all its problems. How bad could church be anyway? I remember going a couple times with my mom when I was growing up and it wasn't too bad: just a bunch of crappy music, dressed up old people and time to sleep.

"May I ask why?" I was startled from my thoughts once again by Pops' voice.

"Why what?" I had already detached myself too far from the conversation to realize what he was asking me.

"Sam saw him rowing in today," Gran responded for me.

Oh, I thought to myself, he was asking why I was wondering about Ben. I liked the thought that Ben had a sadness about him, that drew me to him even more, maybe he could relate, but then a strong jealousy grew, how come he can row out and escape everyday and I'm stuck here? I decided that wasn't fair and was determined to learn to row. I lapped my soup for a little while, trying to decide whether or not to ask about church. Lifting my spoon to my mouth, I blew on the chowder and under my breath asked,

"So, church?"

"Pardon?" my grandparents responded in unison. It was almost comedic.

"I dunno, what's church?" I asked, immediately regretting my choice of words. I know what church is. I more wanted to know about their church.

"We go every Sunday, we sing some hymns, the pastor gives us a message and we were hoping you would come with us, but the choice is yours," answered Gran.

"She left out that after the message she talks to her friends for hours," laughed Pops, which received a stern look from Gran. I couldn't help but let out a slight laugh at the situation.

"Yeah, I guess I'll go check it out."

So, three days later and Sunday was upon us. I woke up to a warm breakfast to share with Pops and Gran. The anticipation I had

31

been feeling for this day had subsided and my heart was racing. I was afraid of meeting all these new people, new faces and awkward situations. I laughed at the irony of it, my deepest longing was just to row out and away from it all, yet here I was, going to the center of all the people to try to find my way out. But I could see from Pops' and Gran's expressions their excitement that I was actually going with them and I figured one Sunday wouldn't kill me. I put on my nicest pair of slacks and my button-up shirt, and Pops tied a tie for me. I didn't own one so he let me wear one of his. I felt very uncomfortable.

We loaded up in the truck and drove the ten-minute drive to church. The church was exactly how I pictured church to be. It was an almost perfectly square structure and all the outside was painted white. Above the doors, there was nailed a cross and there was a small square stained glass window. On both sides of the door were more windows and each side of the building had two stained glass windows. The entry protruded out slightly further than the main front wall of the church and had a smaller roof about seven or eight feet shorter than the main roof. The entry roof had a small square steeple with a triangular roof which was only about three feet tall in total. The large roof was tin and the morning sun shone off the metal brightly, right into my eyes, and I squinted to take in the rest of the scene. At the very front was the main steeple, consisting of two square structures stacked, and the large point rising from those into the sky. I had to admit the church was quaint yet beautiful.

I followed Pops and Gran through the people gathered outside towards the doors to go in. I looked over my shoulder back towards the parking lot and saw Ben. He was standing outside the passenger-side door of an old beat-up car. His big curly brown beard with the reddish tint immediately drew my eyes to him and I realized who it was. He was dressed in a suit and his tie was hanging straight down in front of him as he leaned with one hand on the roof of the car and the other grasped tightly by the elderly lady who was getting out of the car.

The woman had light gray hair which almost seemed completely white and it was messily pulled up into a bun with strands which seemed to be falling out. She wore a dress that appeared to be a dark navy with small white flowers scattered throughout the entire pattern and a long white blouse underneath. The middle of her collar was brought together in a broach which seemed to have an ivory silhouette in the middle. She seemed to be very old, making my grandparents almost seem young. I would later learn that she was 93. As I continued to follow Pops and Gran into the sanctuary, I stole a few more glances back and saw Ben carefully hold one hand while she carried a cane in the other. He walked ever so slowly and gingerly next to her, his entire focus on her every step.

The sanctuary consisted of three aisles, the middle one separating the two rows of pews and one on either side. In front of all the pews was a small stage separated from the rest of the church by an altar and a wooden pulpit. On the right side of the sanctuary, was an old organ, not particularly fancy or consisting of many great pipes, but an organ that looked as though it had stirred chords deep inside the members of the church and had faithfully been there through all the events of the church.

At row three, Pops went down to the far end of the pew and Gran followed. I took my place to the right of Gran. We sat there in silence and I observed the congregation gathering. It wasn't long before Ben slowly walked by, took the elderly lady he was escorting to the front row, and sat next to her. The congregation seemed to be mostly older folks. There were some young families, but there were mostly people who looked like they must have gone there for the better half of the century. Even with the odds stacked against me, I was hoping that a beautiful girl my age would arrive with her family and sit down right next to me. Well, I anxiously waited to no avail and the spot next to me was taken by a man I guessed to be in his 40's, who was perspiring fiercely and breathed as though a mill stone was resting on his chest. I scooted towards Gran.

The pastor was robed in black. By my best estimate he was in his late 50's. He stood before the congregation, welcomed everyone, had us all turn in our hymnals to number 247, and immediately the organ blared through the small church. All around me, people were paging through hymnals. Gran held one open right in front of me and the congregation joined in, "Great is thy faithfulness…"

As everyone sang, I looked around and observed. Gran was holding the hymnal for both of us, but never once looked down to see the words and sang the whole thing by heart. Pops didn't even have a hymnal and sang every word. Everyone in the church seemed to have different habits: Some sang from the book, some held the hymnal but didn't sing, but everyone sang from their heart. I looked up to Ben but wasn't sure whether he was singing or not. I kept thinking I could see his mouth moving from my angle but then would change my mind as the song carried on. I watched intently, partly trying to figure out my own motives.

"…Thine own dear presence to cheer and to guide; Strength for today…" with those words Ben's hand was raised in the air as if he was testifying for something. He must really like those words I thought to myself, "…and bright hope for tomorrow, blessings all mine, with ten thousand beside."

I hated to admit it to myself, but I actually enjoyed the hymn and the way it sounded with the melodious mix of the organ and the congregation's voices. Once the song had ended, the pastor had us all greet one another. The man next to me held out his sweaty hand; I cringed and shook it while the people all around offered me their hands with kind words of welcome. After the greetings, the pastor prayed a prayer of welcome to begin the service. A man from the congregation whose body looked old and frail feebly made his way to stage. I thought the poor man would never make it to the podium, but he did and laid his Bible in front of him. He then pulled glasses out of his chest pocket and took a moment to find his place.

"Therefore I tell you," he intoned. I was shocked, the man's voice was anything but frail. It rang out with conviction and strength, and he spoke in such a way that it shook me to attention. "Do not worry about your life, what you will eat or drink; or about your body, what you will wear. Is not life more important than food, and the body more important than clothes? Look at the birds of the air; they do not sow or reap or store away in barns, and yet your heavenly Father feeds them. Are you not much more valuable than they? Who of you by worrying can add a single hour to his life?"

He closed the Bible and carefully made his way back to his seat. The pastor then stood and took his place at the podium and began his message, his voice more soothing than that of the man who had read the scriptures. But my attention span had run its course. During the entire sermon, I watched around the sanctuary, flipped through the hymnal and thought to myself. The message seemed to drag on, and occasionally I would listen in for a few brief moments, but couldn't bring myself to stay focused. The strange thing was I felt guilty about it, but not guilty enough to listen. Finally the tone of his voice indicated that the end was near and I alerted back up. Next thing I knew, we were going through the hymnal again and sounds of the organ filled the air. "When peace, like a river, attendeth my way," the voices of the congregation joined back in, "when sorrows like sea billows roll; whatever my lot, Thou has taught me to say, It is well, it is well with my soul." The congregation continued with the hymn. I was especially fond of this one; it had a nice ring to it and seemed secure with itself. Ben had his hand raised the entire time. A cast of others would raise or lower theirs at certain parts, but Ben held his strong the entire time. I wondered to myself what that was all about. As soon as the voices ceased, the pastor held both his hands high into the air and commanded us to, "Go in the grace and peace of Jesus Christ.

Immediately, the stillness was gone and the congregation was a mixture of a hustle to gather themselves and head out the door or to find a certain person and begin socializing. I soon realized it was Gran's custom to linger and converse with anyone and everyone who was willing. This first Sunday I was eager to return home. My stomach was growling and I had definitely had my fill of socializing for the week. Little did I know, this was Gran's time to be social for the week. Pops and I leaned against the far wall of the church, observing as people caught up on the week's happenings and made afternoon plans. We watched as Gran joyfully talked to every breathing soul in church that day. As Gran was making her rounds, I watched Ben once again help the elderly lady bundle back up in her jacket and then carefully escort her through the maze of people forming through the church. I looked hard to see what Gran had said about his eyes.

I had a lot of doubt about how could someone have sad eyes? The whole idea of it all seemed absolutely ridiculous to me. He probably was the happiest person there -- he was lucky enough to sail free, without constraints, on the ocean. But as he walked out and I got a good look, for the first time in my life, I understood sad eyes. There seemed to be a sort of heaviness weighing down his brow, the skin underneath the eyes seemed to be marked by years of pain and there was almost a redness about the eyes, not the redness of a drunk or of allergies, but a redness from tears and lack of sleep. The eyes themselves shone as if tears were welled up inside, able to pour out on a moment's notice. But the sadness ended with the eyes, it was as if he had two faces. From the mid-nose to the forehead was a man of pain and sorrow, with a secret. The rest of the face hidden within the bushy beard was a man of joy and warmth. There seemed to be a great mystery to it. I was determined to find out what it was.

When Gran finally was through with her socializing, Pops and I happily joined her on the walk out the door. We returned to the house and had a delicious pot roast Gran had been working on. I don't remember much of what took place the rest of that day because in my mind I was coming up with thousands of reasons why Ben was the way he was, but not a single one made sense to me. It was funny to me that here I was analyzing this man's life and I hadn't even met him.

For the rest of the summer my days were spent relatively the same way. I would wake up early and have breakfast with my grandparents, occasionally read from the old dusty books in my room, but mostly spend my days outside. That first summer Pops set about teaching me all he knew of the land, the sea, the boats, fishing and any and everything else he could think of. Pops would ask me to help with random chores and repairs he had to make around the house and I was always eager to learn how he did something or to see how something worked. Several times Pops invited me to accompany him in the truck on errands, chores and sometimes just pleasure drives around the state. I loved these times, just Pops, me and the truck. We would put our windows down and have the radio playing loudly. My eyes were always glued to the scenery and different sights which were all so new to me.

No matter what I was doing I would always try to catch Ben rowing out in the morning and making his way back to the harbor at night. Sometimes I would stand on the point clearly visible so he would see me, and every time he did he would offer a head nod or a wave. My reasoning behind this was if he saw me, he might think I was interested in boating or offer to show me how to row. I knew this was desperate thinking but I longed to go out to sea and leave the world behind. Other times I would hide behind a tree and peer off the porch.

It was also during those fading summer days that conversation with Pops and Gran grew easier for me, but I still had the habit I despised of getting openly mad at them for no good reason, punishing them and occasionally even yelling at them. They always responded with love and understanding. They never pushed me and dropped most things as soon I started trying to make a big deal about them. Never at the time would I have realized it, but I was slowly beginning a painful season of change in my life. There were many more steps which had to fall in place, but the chain of events had been set in motion.

In the fall, I began classes at the local high school and my days became very different. I decided that since people were the source of all of the pain in my life, I would try to go the entire year without talking to anyone. In hindsight, it was a miserable goal but remembering it reminds me of the pain I felt during those early years. The few blessed souls who tried to befriend me or even just talk to me, quickly changed their minds with my cold, sharp responses to their inquiries. This was another habit I hated. At this point I really wanted nothing more to just blend in, have a group of friends, live like everyone else seemed to be, enjoying life with no worry. I wanted to belong and just be normal, but my pain caused me to isolate myself and every time a brave person would attempt to befriend me and I would shoot them down, my heart would ache. I felt as though my pain was causing me to self destruct. The worst was when people would ask where I came from. Just that phrase brought back too many painful memories, and often times I wouldn't respond, I would just glare. Needless to say, I didn't win any awards for most popular that year.

During the first semester of high school, the weather made the change from the warm summer days to the cool fall. The splendor of the trees was absolutely beautiful and there was crispness about the air. I loved to close my eyes and linger on a deep breath. It was always after these moments when I would laugh to myself and realize how I was becoming like Pops in that aspect. Then the weather changed from fall to the fierce and bitter winter, the cold was strong and snow came. It was during these cold winter months that nights were spent near the fireplace, Gran knitting, Pops reading or doing his daily crossword and I either working on homework or reading excerpts from some of the old books in my room. I was always embarrassed to read in front of Pops and Gran, but for some reason these books just called out to me. I couldn't leave them be on that shelf. But as much as I really did enjoy them it didn't change the fact that my attention span wasn't long enough to read a good portion.

Sitting around the fireplace, I felt a sense of belonging in an environment of safety I had not known before in my life. Gran would always get up and either put on some coffee, tea and the occasional mug of hot cocoa. Sometimes we would sit there with our respective distractions and yet just hold them in our laps and engage in conversation, and other times we would say nothing at all. I grew to love either situation, and it seemed as though they came with just the right timing and amount. If I didn't have a constant distraction my mind would wander. During that first fall and winter in Maine, these moments occurred in a much higher frequency when I didn't have the distraction of the outdoors. Visions of my past would come to me or I would think how my mom didn't even miss me. I was sure she was even happier with me gone. One Sunday I decided not to go to church with Pops and Gran and the entire time they were gone, I was tormented by my thoughts and my past seemed to constantly scream back into memory. I never again missed a Sunday.

The other new phenomena that began to occur that summer were dreams. I never quite understood them and couldn't really place why they occurred, but they were constant companions that first summer. I wouldn't always remember them, sometimes just the fact that I had dreamed would come to mind. But there were some I remember. One in particular is vivid to this day.

I am sneaking out to the boat house. Pops is gone and Gran has fallen asleep knitting. There *Santiago* is sitting and calling to me. I use all the force and might I have to get it down the ramp into the water. I place the oars in their locks and push off the shore and out to the water. As soon as I am in the water, a strong current pulls me far out to sea, and I remember watching the coastline shrink farther and farther away. There is a strong mix of feeling between the elation of finally escaping the real world and a deep fear of not being able to control where I am going. I desperately struggle to gain control of the oars and steer myself but I never can. Then the sky in a moment turns black and winds come from all directions. The *Santiago* is tossed about and I brace myself in the frame of the boat. I can hear the oars ripped from their locks. The rain soaks through my clothes and I shiver as I hold on for dear life. My eyes are closed tight and the noise of the heavy rain and raging winds mixed with the crashing waves and the creaking of the old boat are all I can hear. I feel the boat rise high in the air as it slowly turns port side and a roller crashes completely over and next thing I know I am capsized and startled awake.

I'll never forget how relieved I was to wake up while at the same time very disappointed to be back in my normal life. Such dreams became routine as the winter passed slowly on but whenever I would seem down, Gran would look at me with a sweet smile and remind me spring was just around the corner.

Before spring could arrive we had the festivities of Christmas. I'll never forget that first Christmas in Maine. I welcomed the break from school eagerly and enjoyed the smell of the fir tree we had selected for our Christmas tree that year. There wasn't a really big deal made on Christmas day itself: We woke up and had breakfast together and then we went to the tree. Pops and Gran exchanged their gifts. Pops got Gran some knitting thread and needles and Gran had stitched a sweater for Pops. I laughed aloud at that. Then Gran had made a sweater for me that I wore constantly that winter, it was so warm. Pops handed me a small package in brown paper, tied with a simple string. I opened it, a first edition of *The Old Man and the Sea* by Ernest Hemingway. Pops looked at me with a wink and said, "You'll love it."

He was right; that was the fastest I had read through a book in my life. I immediately was so envious of both Santiago and the boy. I understood why Pops had named the rowboat after Santiago and I longed to be able to escape to the sea more than ever before. In fact, I read the book through twice before I returned to school the next January. Every day that passed during the remainder of that winter, I grew more and more excited. As the snow melted and the weather slowly grew warmer, new life began to spring up all around us. A little bit of new life was beginning to bud up within me, but it would take the most interesting summer of my life to prepare the soil for what was in store.

THREE

After months of my staring out the window, watching the snow slowly melt and life return to the surrounding flora and fauna, summer had finally arrived. I left the high school that last day having successfully avoided making any real friendships for an entire year and I took great pride in that fact. Summer was finally here and I had big ambitions for this particular summer. I was determined that it would not end before I had learned how to row and had gone out in the *Santiago* on my own. The sense of that future freedom was exhilarating, and I knew I would be able to spend the wondrous days of summer with no responsibilities, just enjoying the outdoors.

The first morning of summer, I woke up at the usual time to share breakfast with Pops and Gran. I had already planned that I would ask to take one of the old kayaks out for the day. The scene had evolved perfectly in my mind's eye: I would ask Pops, who would eagerly agree that it was a great idea. Gran might even pack me a lunch to eat out on the water so I wouldn't have to come back for it. I would row out and spend the day exploring the entire bay. I would stay away from the harbor where there was definitely too much civilization for me. I would stay out until the sun was beginning to set, and Pops would see I was such a natural that the next day he would show me how to use *Santiago* and then every day for the rest of the summer I would row out. Well, things never seem to go as I plan them in my mind. Just when I was finally building up my courage and just when I was about to ask Pops for permission, he beat me to it.

"Say, Sam, I notice you seem fond of Ben." As Pops spoke those words, I was embarrassed. The way he phrased it made me feel childish, even though I knew this wasn't his intent. He continued, "Well, I was talking to him the other day and he said he could use a hand doing his work this summer. I told him I would talk to you and see what you thought. How does that sound?"

The whole thing caught me unprepared. Abruptly, the dream of endless days of exploring and rowing were replaced with the vision of days of work and routine. My desire for entire days without interaction with people was replaced with the dread of constant interaction. At first, no, the idea didn't sit well with me at all. I stared down blankly at my oatmeal.

The first person to break the silence was Gran. "That would be nice. Ben would be a great guy to work with and I'm sure he'd become a great friend. It would be nice to have something to do, so you wouldn't be so bored all the time, right, Sam?"

Who the hell had said I was bored all the time or that I even wanted a friend? I immediately felt bad for the instinctive response, especially to Gran, even if it was only in my mind. I knew they were just trying to be nice, but it is a difficult thing to have made plans and goals and then have someone who thinks they're looking out for you, make other plans for you behind your back. They both were staring at me, waiting for my response. I hated to let them down. I really hadn't decided what I thought of it, either. I didn't mind work, and I had really enjoyed the projects I had helped Pops with last summer. But what did Ben even do for work? To me, it seemed like he was always out at sea. Suddenly, my heart began to beat fast. Maybe this was my chance. Maybe he would take me out with him every day and maybe I would learn the way of the sea and then maybe I could go out on my own.

My curiosity was too much. "What work does Ben even do?"

"Well, he's a handy man of sorts," Pops began to clarify. "He pretty much does anything: wood working, work on property or houses. Fishes a lot, too. I'm not completely sure what he had in mind, to be honest with you, Sam, but I'm sure it'll have enough variety to keep you interested. How about you think about it today and let me know tonight and then I'll give him a call?"

"Okay, will do."

That definitely seemed like the best option to me. Immediately after breakfast I went for a walk, found a perfect spot between some pines to lie down and lay on my back thinking. The sound of a far off loon interrupted my peace, but I didn't mind. I was fond of the loons and proud that I could recognize a bird call. Pops and Gran loved the birds; they could name any bird we ever spotted without looking at a book. Sometimes I would be on the porch with Gran and no birds would be visible but a call would be heard and just by the call, she would recognize what kind it was.

I was really torn by the whole situation. Pops had mentioned that Ben did a lot of fishing; maybe that's what he needed help with. I pictured it like Santiago and the boy in *The Old Man and the Sea*. I wouldn't mind that at all. Unfortunately, when I tried to weigh my options, all I could picture was its being just like Hemingway's book and I made little progress. Finally, as I was lying there, I decided to take the job. I figured that in the worst case scenario, I would hate it and quit. Well, I lay there the rest of the morning, my hands behind my head, my eyes closed and I slowly drifted off.

I dream of my mom. This dream is different than any I have ever had before. She is in a courtroom and being questioned. She stands on one side and I am on the other. She has a lawyer who is whispering in her ear and telling her how to answer the judge's interrogations. I grow angry; they are all questions about me and where I belong. She completely denies even knowing me. A boiling anger and immense sadness are welling up inside me. I stare at my mom and try to scream out for her to ignore her lawyer and notice me, but every time I try, no words come out. Suddenly the lawyer looks towards me. It is my stepdad. He smiles and as he does, the judge slams the gavel and declares my mom free of me. Suddenly a trap door opens beneath me. Before I begin to fall, I frantically look all around and no one is there in my defense. Pops and Gran are seated in the front row and they are crying, but they can't reach out and help me. Then I begin to fall.

"Soup's on!" Gran's shout aroused me from my slumber. Extremely startled but glad to be awakened from the dream, I sat up and rested my weight on my arms behind me. Blinking several times as my eyes adjusted to the midday sun, I got to my feet and brushed the pine needles off my legs and headed for the house. The dream had put me in sort of a funk, but it was a funk unlike ones I had been in before. My mind struggled to determine if anyone ever would stand in my defense. It felt pretty hopeless. It is amazing me to this day the power a dream could have over my mood. Back at the house, it was a joy to be in the presence of people -- and that is definitely something that I couldn't or wouldn't say very often in my early years in Maine.

Gran had made chicken salad sandwiches and we had some sea-salt and vinegar potato chips. I stared out the window, just looking at the trees. For the moment I wished I was a tree, to have no feelings, no emotions, yet to be so strong and unmovable. As I was staring at a far-off birch, a small bird landed on one of the branches. She hopped from branch to branch and then froze momentarily before flying off and out of sight. Why couldn't I even be a bird, I wondered to myself, to be able to just fly away from everything whenever I so desired? Life would be so much less complicated and I would have so much freedom.

Picking up my sandwich, I took a bite and in my head cursed my humanity. Pops was going on about some fungus he had seen on a walk earlier which had fascinated him. I was half listening and half daydreaming. I'm pretty sure Gran was listening intently and was just as fascinated as Pops was. For a moment I wished I was a fungus and people were fascinated with me, but I quickly dismissed that idea, and was glad I was a human. When they had exhausted the story of the newly discovered treasure, I decided the moment was prime for my announcement.

"I'll work with Ben," I kind of mumbled under my breath, not sure if they even heard me.

"Well that's excellent!" beamed Gran with a smile.

"What's excellent, Dear?" Pops obviously hadn't heard me.

"That Sam will be working with Ben this summer."

"We don't know that yet."

"He just said so." Her frustration was beginning to show.

"Oh, well, that's wonderful!" Pops finally exclaimed.

I couldn't help it, I began to chuckle at the entire conversation and before I knew it Pops and Gran were both laughing along. It was one of those good healthy laughs where once you begin, you just continue on and on. The thing which originally got you laughing in the first place no longer seems that funny to you, but you can't stop laughing. We were all on the verge of tears, and the dream from this afternoon was far from my memory.

After we finished eating, I helped Gran with the dishes and Pops went into the other room to give Ben a call. In hindsight, even if I didn't realize it at the moment, I always enjoyed my time with Pops and Gran. I also very much enjoyed one-on-one time with either of them. I longed to ask so many questions of both her and Pops, but every time the opportunity arose, I seemed unable to get the words out. I wondered about my father, about what could've been, how things ended up the way they did, how he was raised. This was just such an opportunity with Gran. Gran was drying today and as I was washing, I kept looking over to her, trying to form the words, my mouth making the shapes, but the words never came out. I longed for her to look up and see me and then ask what I was trying to say, but every time she looked up, my lips would seal shut, almost beyond my control. So, we just stood there, washing and drying, and humming a beautiful song. As the pile of dirty dishes shrank, my courage to ask grew and finally, I could resist no longer. I didn't care; I would just ask. The warmth of the sun shining through the window felt wonderful, and I put my hands on the edge of the kitchen sink.

"Hey, Gran," I started, but just as I began to ask, the moment was lost.

"Well, you begin tomorrow, Sam!" Pops came back into the room.

I was disappointed. I was about to finally pose the questions to Gran and now the chance was gone and I had lost all desire to ask. Immediately nerves came, and I was worried about work the next day. Never before in my life had I ever had a paying job or done real work. This would be an entirely new experience and I had no idea what to expect. What should I wear? What would I be doing? Would I even be able to do what I was required to do? I didn't even really know Ben. I wondered, would he be nice, would he understand? Suddenly, I just pictured his asking me all about my past and I began to get angry just thinking about it. Any joy I had at the prospect was now completely gone and it was replaced with extreme anxiety and dread.

"Aren't you excited, Sam?" Gran must have noticed my silence.

47

"I just don't know what to expect."

"You'll be fine, Sam, trust me. Ben knows you are new at it and he's a great guy. He won't make it too hard. He said he was going to help bricking a house. He'll pick you up at six tomorrow morning."

"Six?" I interrupted.

"Yeah, a good healthy work day. He said he'll teach you everything you need to know."

Pops must have thought that would be reassuring to me, but I was too far gone for it to help. Who else would be there, would they make fun of me? I could just picture their asking me to do things and my not having any idea how or what to do. Why six in the morning, too? I don't mind mornings, but six? Bricking a house sounded hard and if I messed up, I was sure it would be quite obvious. I could just picture myself being completely responsible for an entire house falling down.

So, doing what was habit for me in those days, when things brought me down, I went back out, down to the point and sat on the rocks. An osprey was circling overhead with its bent wings. I looked around trying to see if it had a nest high in any of the surrounding pines, but I couldn't see anything. The ocean was especially calm, with hardly a wave or ripple. I dangled my feet in the water and the cold chill gave me goose bumps. Kicking my feet back and forth in the sea, I leaned back on my hands, the warm stone offsetting the chill of the water. I could see a motorboat kicking up wake as it made its way out to sea and far off I could see the triangular white sail of a sailboat. I looked out at the islands in the bay. Scattered around the rocky shores, fishermen were enjoying a relaxing day of fishing.

Early the next morning I got out of bed, incredibly tired and wishing for nothing more than a few more hours of sleep. It took all of my effort to get dressed, but I made sure I was ready -- I didn't want to be late on my first day of work. Downstairs, Gran had a hot breakfast prepared for me. I wasn't expecting her to do this and it was a very pleasant surprise. As I ate my share of cheesy scrambled eggs, warm buttery toast, and crunchy bacon, Gran sat at the table sipping a cup of hot coffee. Slightly before six, we heard a honk and I looked outside to see Ben's beat-up old truck. Gran handed me a packed lunch and a large thermos of coffee. She really did take good care of me.

I opened the door to find Ben standing there. He was wearing a T-shirt, jeans, a brown jacket, and a handsome pair of boots. His bushy brown beard with its subtle hint of red still attracted my attention; it encircled a beaming smile which contrasted with his sad and tired eyes. He greeted me with a firm handshake and Gran with a hug. She handed him a packed lunch, which he graciously accepted, and we made our way to his truck as I prepared for my first day of work.

We each sipped coffee as he drove to the worksite. This was the moment of truth; I wondered if the pedestal I had been holding him up on would crumble beneath him. I was nervous. I was pulling for Ben to live up to all of my assumptions and hopes. As much as I hated to admit it to myself, I was nervous; yes, my anxiety about the work was masked by the anxiety about the ride there with Ben. I sat there in silence. I had nothing to say and it would have been fine with me if nothing had been said at all. The aroma of coffee in the truck was very relaxing. Ben held his thermos to his lips, took a deep gulp. He wiped his lips with the upper part of his jacket sleeve and then he broke the silence, "How do you like your coffee?"

His voice caught me by surprise I had always pictured a husky, deep voice that would silence everything else when he spoke, but this wasn't the case. It was very typical, not a voice that would stand out in a crowd. The question was harmless enough in itself as well. No deep prodding questions about my past. I wanted him to like me though and having no idea why, I figured I would try a small dose of humor.

"Well I started off drinking a little coffee with my cream and sugar, but now I can drink it black, but prefer cream." I said with a laugh that sounded like a rush of air being expelled from my lungs.

"I know what you mean. It's definitely an acquired taste. I think still hated coffee when I was your age and now I live by it."

I wanted to say something in response, anything. I just wanted him to know that I enjoyed talking and that I was trying. I prodded my mind and in frustration, everything I could come up with seemed stupid or trivial so I sat there in silence. By the time I actually thought of a response the appropriate time for a response was long gone, so I just took another sip of my coffee. After several minutes of driving north Ben finally broke the silence once more.

"Have you ever done any masonry or any construction type work?"

"No, I haven't gotten a chance to do much in that area." I didn't want him to think I hadn't worked any at all before.

"Alright, well, you'll be fine. I told a friend I would brick a house for him. I used to work for a mason during the summers in college, so I'll be laying and you'll be mixing. I'll show you the ropes when we get there. It's not too complicated. We'll probably be working on this house for the rest of the week.

I have a good start but it's hard to mix and lay all at the same time."

"Sounds good to me."

"It's hard work but it's fun, a lot better than sitting in an office all day, if you ask me."

As he spoke, he stared straight ahead at the winding road. Every time his mouth moved even slightly, it was magnified by the hairs of his upper lip and chin. While he spoke, he seemed to have a grin on his face and whenever he stopped speaking, it was gone. But how could his eyes be so incredibly different? The sharp contrast made it look as though he had some kind of eye disease, giving him a tired and even sad appearance no matter the circumstances.

The drive was only about fifteen minutes, and for a majority of the time, we listened to country music on the radio. At this point in my life, country was a taste I had not yet acquired, but Ben seemed to be a big fan. I would occasionally look over and see his lips moving with the words to a song. I wondered had I not been in the truck if he would have burst out singing. While we were driving along the coast, I spent most of the ride staring out the window as the tree line gave way to a rocky coast. The sea looked magnificent and the gulls flying overhead seemed so free and careless. I wondered if I would ever get even a taste of that feeling. As we neared the house, I started getting nervous; I began to realize I had no idea what I was getting myself into and that scared me. Finally, Ben pulled into a dirt drive, and there it was.

The house was a small ranch. There was dirt all around and the house was covered in white Tyvek house wrap. The far side of the house, with a chimney, was completely bricked and the corners were hung to join the opposite side, checkerboard fashion. All around the house, bricks were stacked in columns probably four feet tall. The front was completely covered by scaffolding and there were buckets and other sorts of material lying randomly around the whole work site.

"We'll be working on the front today," Ben explained as he hopped out of the truck and slammed the door. He motioned me over to a large metal mixer of sorts and explained that this was where I would be mixing the mortar. It was painted in what at one time could have been a bright yellow, but was now a very soft mustard shade, mostly covered by old mortar and dust. It looked like a large barrel laid on its side with the top cut open and a cage that swung up and down with a lip to pour the mortar when the barrel was rolled to its side. On the same platform was a motor that looked much like the motors on lawnmowers, with a gas tank and a pull cord. Under the motor, the whole contraption was held on two tires and opposite those, a trailer hitch held it all level. I assumed this machine was older than I and that it had been mixing mortar for many years. I peered down into the barrel and saw a mixer which must turn when the machine was running. I thought it would be fun to learn how this whole thing worked. Next to it was a large hill of sand with a shovel stuck in it. Stacks of mortar powder were piled on top of a nearby wooden palette, lined up and packed in plastic.

After I had looked into the mixer and surveyed the house for a little bit, Ben asked me to help him unload the truck. Strapped in the back of his truck were two 50-gallon barrels of water. We brought another barrel over from the back of the house, this one empty. We placed the empty barrel at the tailgate of his truck and tipped over one of the first barrels in the truck until water filled the empty one. We unloaded them all in the same fashion. Already I had worked more in this day than any other time before in my life, so I felt very satisfied. Ben jumped in the bed of his truck and threw out several 5-gallon buckets and an orange device that I assumed must be used to hold bricks. My assumption was proven true, as Ben told me it was a brick tong.

During the day, Ben showed me the ropes, which were difficult ropes. We spent what seemed like years moving bricks from the piles throughout the yard onto scaffolding placed along the side of the house so that once we began laying, the work would go smoothly. This process involved picking up stacks of 11 bricks in the tongs, carrying them to the scaffolding and then figuring out how to climb the scaffolding with one hand and hold the tongs in the other. Needless to say, I spent a lot of time picking out of the dirt below all the bricks I had dropped. Ben moved two to three times as many bricks as I did. By the time the scaffolding was full, my hands, shoulders, arms and back were stiff and aching. My hand was scratched and slightly bloodied from picking up the bricks that fell out of my tongs. Sweat was dripping off every surface of my body and the work was just beginning.

We worked the morning mostly in silence, with Ben making an occasional joke or singing under his breath. I didn't have the breath to talk or joke. I didn't even hear the rhythmic beating of the pileated woodpecker from the nearby woods or see the northern cardinal perched on the chimney looking curiously on. About midmorning, Ben walked over to the cab of his truck and pulled out two water bottles, one of which he tossed to me. Thanking him, I eagerly drank up the sweet cool refreshment. Ben never seemed to tire; he worked hard, really hard. I couldn't understand why he worked so hard, especially with no one watching him or supervising him. I wondered what he gained from working like that?

Before I knew it, my water was gone and it was back to work. We went over to the old mixer into which Ben poured five gallons of water. He went over to its lawn-motor-like engine and pulled the cord. The old machine let out a few delayed putters, but Ben wiped the sweat from his brow with the rolled up sleeve on his forearm, gave another hard tug and the machine roared into action. The large stirring device within the barrel of the machine began to spin and toss the water around. Ben grabbed a bag of the cement powder and with a thrust of his knee tossed it upon the grated cage, cutting a hole in the bag. Pulling up on both sides the powder fell into the water. The dark gray mixture was thrown about but still had the consistency of water. Then Ben began to heave shovel after shovel of sand into the mixture, occasionally pausing to watch as the sand disappeared into the ever thickening concoction. When he had determined it was the perfect consistency, he unhinged the barrel and lowered it, spilling the mixture into the waiting wheelbarrow. He then took his trowel, scrapped the excess from the lip and returned the barrel.

"Toss some water in there to keep what's left from drying on us."

He wheeled the mud to the scaffolding as I filled a five-gallon bucket and poured it into the mixer. The roar of the engine was really more than I could handle, and I looked forward to learning how to turn the machine off.

"This mud should last us 'til lunch."

Ben was shoveling the mud from the barrel to the wooden slabs set between the blocks of wood on the scaffolding. With what appeared to be an easy heave, he thrust the head of the shovel up and the mud poured perfectly on the wood.

"Just make sure there is always plenty of mud and we'll be in business."

With that Ben started to lay the brick. If you ever get a chance to watch an experienced brick layer, don't pass it up, for it is their art and after years of practice they develop a sense and skill for it that seems to come very naturally. For the first several minutes, I stood by the wheel barrel and watched as Ben would pick up a brick and scoop up the mud with his trowel. As if he were icing a cake, he would lay the mud on the spot where the brick was to go and on the opposite ends of the brick, then he would place the brick and use the trowel to clear the excess mud and continue on. It seemed to come so fluidly and before I knew it, both the pile of bricks and the mound of mud waiting to get used had shrunk before my very eyes and needed replenishing.

I took the shovel and scooped it down in the wheel barrel and pulled with all my might to lift it above my head in the same way Ben had done when he had originally loaded the scaffold, but as I raised the shovel above me, I heard the mud come splashing down onto the dirt below. Ben just laughed it off and promised that with time I would get it down. Until then, he told me to relay the mud to the boards using the five-gallon buckets.

I spent the afternoon in seemingly constant motion, keeping bricks and mud supplied while Ben kept laying them down. I struggled when it was my turn to mix the mud: The first batch I tried was too runny. Nervous Ben would get upset, I hesitated to tell him I needed help, but he was eager and kind in helping and mixed in some more sand and a little powder to his liking and got back to work. It was hot and I had cement everywhere, all over my clothes and sweat was pouring onto the dirt. I couldn't imagine how Ben was able to stand that beard; it looked as though it would increase his body temperature by 50 degrees. But Ben never complained about the heat or anything else for that matter.

After he had used all of two wheelbarrows of mud, Ben decided it was time for lunch. The Tyvek wrap covering the front of the house was slowly disappearing and with every bit that disappeared, my appetite and thirst grew. We got Gran's lunches from the truck and sat on the lowered tail gate of Ben's truck while we ate. At first, the initial hunger seemed to overtake us and we avoided conversation but a couple of minutes later, when Ben had satisfied his hunger enough to be able to eat and converse at the same time, we initiated conversation.

"So, what do you think of it? Dream job?" he asked with a smile.

"Its work, that's for sure."

"You've got that right," he said, his eyes in a distant gaze and still glazed over with sadness even when joking. He continued on, "So when you're not filling your time working or at school, what do you like to do?"

Immediately reading came to mind and I was mad. Why the hell did reading come to mind? Yes, I read and I guess I enjoyed it, but I didn't want reading to be the first thing that came to mind when asked what I liked to do for fun, no less. I hesitated, nature! That was it.

"I love nature. I love just walking around Pops' and Gran's property. I could spend all day just exploring and being outside."

"They do have a nice place there. You like the water? Ever get to use that old boat of your Grandpa's? She sure is a beauty."

He knew about *Santiago*; maybe this was my chance, maybe he would understand my longing. As afraid as I was at open up to someone, I couldn't help it. I wanted to learn to row.

"I love the water," I blurted out, embarrassed at showing that much emotion. "Pops hasn't gotten around to showing me how to row, but I can't wait until I can take out the *Santiago*."

"The *Santiago*, I like that, classic Hemingway."

Obviously Ben was a reader, or at least knew *The Old Man and the Sea*, but had he missed my point, that I wanted to learn how to row and wasn't getting the chance?

"I love the water, too," he continued. "I could spend all day and night out there and not have a second thought."

That's what I want, that's my dream, my longing was screaming inside of me. It felt as though he knew it and was teasing and taunting me. Surely he wouldn't do that, would he? But why was he talking about how he loved to escape and not offering me the same chance? Had I given Ben the benefit of the doubt only to realize it was a waste? I dreaded thinking so.

"You know, I go out about every weekend."

Of course I knew that. I had watched him go out and return, and it had seemed to me that he went out almost daily. Saying "about every weekend" really seemed to downplay the amount of time he spent on the ocean. I was glad he never brought up seeing me on the rock, watching him row out and return after a long day. The very thought of it was embarrassing to me. Then his voice interrupted my thoughts.

"Would you want to go with me this Saturday? I could probably teach you a thing or two about rowing."

I could feel myself smiling and that made me mad. Why was I showing all this emotion? But I couldn't kid myself: that was exactly what I had wanted and what I had hoped he would ask when I answered his question. Nonetheless, I played it cool.

"Yeah, I guess that'd be fun. I wouldn't mind it."

"Well, we can set the plans when it gets closer, but now it's time to work." Ben tossed the trash into the bed of his truck; wiped his beard with his wrist, avoiding the dry cement and dirt on his hands; and just like that we were back at work, with the noise of the mixer drowning out the lingering calm from lunch. My excitement for the upcoming weekend was drowned out by the pain and work, and the rest of the day seemed to last forever. I'm sure I checked my watch about every minute until I swore off checking the time and put the watch in the cab of the truck. Finally, when the last barrel of mud had been used and Ben decided we had done enough for the day, I collapsed into the passenger seat.

At moments like those, I usually appreciate the length of summer days, when I am able to go home and enjoy the outdoors before night. This day, Ben dropped me off, gave a honk and a wave to Pops and Gran and drove off, while my sore body struggled into the house. After answering Pops' and Gran's endless questions about the day, I excused myself and went out back. Once again, I felt bad for being short and agitated with Pops and Gran. They just wanted to know how my day was, but I was so frustrated with all the hard work and just so generally agitated that once again they paid the price. I lay there as the day cooled and the shadows of the trees seemed to grow and grow until they encompassed the entire field of vision as night descended. Gradually, my own feelings cooled and peace descended on me as well.

Normally, we had dinner before nightfall and suddenly the thought crossed my mind that it was odd Gran had never called me to come back in. Immediately I was angry: I had had a hard day and deserved dinner more than anyone else, so why would they do this to me? The joy and pleasures of the lazy evening outside instantly dissipated and once again feelings of anger and frustration took their place. I got up and made my way to the house surprised to find nobody on the front porch, a place where both Pops and Gran would usually be found after dinner, reading, doing crosswords or sipping a cup of coffee and enjoying the sunset. It was dark inside too -- very odd unless they had already gone to bed. Entering the house I found them both in their lounge chairs, head back, eyes closed and mouths open. Gran had her latest novel open on her lap and Pops had the newspaper folded on his lap.   Suddenly my feelings melted away, and I remembered they were human just like me. They looked so peaceful, just sleeping there and I couldn't imagine how long they had been that way. Not sure what course of action to take, I decided I would just sit there and wait for one of them to wake up. Now I really was enjoying a truly serene moment, but as I sat and took it in, I realized that I was incredibly hungry and I believe my subconscious was trying to wake them. I noticed my foot kept tapping against the corner table, and I couldn't help but clear my throat. It wasn't long before Pops was startled awake, looking around very confused before he finally got his bearings.

"Goodness sakes, how long have we been out for? I worked up quite the appetite, sleeping," he said, speaking not so much to me as just generalizing his thoughts aloud. "Gran, wake up before the men of the household starve."

That did the trick and Gran quickly joined him in the dazed post-nap state, except that hers was one of regret and I believe she felt terrible that she had slept through dinner. She quickly rose to remedy the situation and as she disappeared into the kitchen, Pops sleepily rubbed his eyes.

"Well, by the looks of it, you would think Gran and I were the ones who started bricking today," he said with a thin smile. I let out a breath through my nostrils the way you do when you find something not as funny as it was intended to be, but don't want the joke teller to be offended.

"Soup's on!" Gran yelled from the kitchen.

"Dang!" Pops responded, "What are we having?   Fast-onion soup?"

59

I didn't even give him a courtesy laugh for that one, but that didn't seem to bother him as he found humor it in anyway. I followed him into the kitchen and as my eyes fell on the spread Gran had laid out for us, my heart fell. I was ravenous after my first day on the job and it was bad enough I had to wait so long for dinner, which wasn't a big deal until now, but all she had just laid out were lunchmeat and condiments for sandwiches. Really? That was going to be dinner? By way of expressing disapproval without actually saying anything, I made a quick sandwich and sat down to begin eating before Pops and Gran had theirs. Not once did I look up from my meal or speak a word during dinner. Whenever a question was asked of me, I would respond by barely moving my shoulders or head to find the proper nonverbal response. When I had finished, I quickly excused myself and went to my room where I proceeded to punch my pillow in fury to get the frustration out, but the day soon caught up with me, and shortly I was asleep.

I am walking down a dark path and a ton of bricks falls on me.

The next day, I woke up not knowing if it had been a dream or reality.

This day went much the same as the day before. Things came slightly easier and the work didn't seem quite so hard, but nonetheless I was still utterly exhausted at the end of the day. As the week went along, I got more and more used to the work and finally, after a long day, on Thursday we completed the house. It is hard to describe the feeling of satisfaction you get seeing a house you have been bricking receive its last brick, but it is a good feeling.

Conversations with Ben during the week never drifted past the superficial and never challenged either of us. I was very happy for that, still pleased that he never once asked me about my past. I returned the favor, as hard as it was seeing those distant sad eyes, almost seeming to hide behind the great bushy beard. As we were cleaning the worksite that Thursday he threw an opportunity I had been waiting for right into my hands.

"Since we're finished here, would you be interested in going with me out rowing tomorrow?"

My adrenaline began to pump and my heart raced. This, finally, was the chance I had been waiting for. "Yeah, that sounds great." My casual answer did not even give a hint of the excitement I was feeling.

"I'll talk to Loring tonight and see if he would let us take out *Santiago* so you can learn on a boat you'll actually use."

Even better, I thought. I had images of my mastering rowing the very first day and then going out and escaping, being alone every chance I got after that. Finally my life would get better, finally I would be free. Maybe I could even quit working with Ben and just go out to sea every day. For the entire drive back home, I was off, thinking of all the opportunities that were sure to open to me once I could row and take the rowboat out. We got back and sure enough, Pops said he would be thrilled if we used *Santiago* and so the countdown began.

We set the time for the next morning and Ben left for home. Pops, Gran and I had dinner and I was more talkative and generally happier than I had been all week. They did not mention this, but they did take advantage of it. It was the kind of night that I love, because I really do enjoy having people care and that night I didn't get mad once. It felt very much like Christmas Eve, and later I lay in bed for seemingly hours until finally I drifted off into a state of excited sleep.

FOUR

I woke up before my alarm, before the sun rose and prepared for the big day ahead. I could already hear the crackling of the bacon in the skillet as Gran prepared breakfast. Above the cooking bacon, I could hear Gran's sweet humming, always songs and tunes I had never heard before. Pops would whistle along, which was mostly pleasant, sometimes even entertaining at times, but at other times he would just about drive me nuts with his loud shrill tunes. But with Gran, there was just something relaxing and peaceful about the way she hummed. She really seemed carefree and happy, qualities I was always envious of. Unsure of what to wear my first day rowing, I just threw on my swimming trunks and a t-shirt. I rushed down the stairs to fill myself with cheesy eggs, bacon and perfectly buttered, toasted English muffin bread. I was surprised to see Ben already there, wiping coffee from his mustache.

"Morning Sam," they all said, unintentionally, in unison, followed by their looking at each other and laughing, which really creeped me out.

"You're up early," was all I could muster to say to Ben. It felt mean and I immediately regretted the harsh remark for the only man who would help me chase my dream. He didn't seem bothered by it.

"I never sleep," he replied and by the look of his eyes, I didn't doubt that for a second. What was bothering him? How did he always have a smile with such a sad aurora about him? These questions plagued me briefly, but I quickly recovered. I didn't care what had happened to him, he didn't need to know my stuff, and I liked it that way. Pops came in from the other room carrying the newspaper under his arm and his beloved Boston mug in his hand (Gran had bought that

62

mug on a family vacation when they were dating). We all sat at the table and enjoyed Gran's breakfast. Conversation was mostly confined to Pops, Gran and Ben; I was pleased to remain silent and just listen. Occasionally one of them would ask me something in an obvious attempt to make me feel included, but I would respond with one of my one word answers or shrugs. Eagerly waiting to hit the water, I began to be annoyed by their love of conversation and grew very irritated. Luckily, it wasn't long before Gran, seemingly reading my mind, decided we were wasting the morning.

"Well, you boys don't want to waste the day away in boring chatter," which was exactly how it felt to me, "Go ahead and seize the sea."

"Seize the sea." It rang pleasantly in my ears. That was precisely my dream and what I wanted to do. Gran remained in the kitchen, happily cleaning up the dishes from breakfast as Pops, Ben and I went out to the boathouse to launch the *Santiago*. It annoyed me that Pops was helping us. Yes, it was his boat, but he hadn't given me a chance to learn it earlier, and now suddenly he was so eager to help someone help me. Pops unlocked the rusty old lock hanging on the big doors, Ben and I swung them open, and there it was, the *Santiago*. Finally my ticket to escape, my way out of the world of people and problems, was here. With its dark forest green sides and the sharp white trim, it was a handsome boat. I saw the way Pops looked at that boat with such pride, a look of great satisfaction. I wanted so badly to be able to look at anything with so much pleasure and contentment. For a moment I did some soul searching, trying to find anything I would look at like that, but it got depressing so I quit.

Ben grabbed the bow and pulled the boat out. I went around to the stern and we moved it to the end of the slip leading over the rocks on the shore line, next to which was a crude boat ramp -- crude by way of looks but well put together. We put the boat on the ramp, and using the rope on the bow, Ben pulled it into the water and along the edge of the slip and tied it up. We gathered the oars, placed the oarlocks in the rowboat, and threw in two life jackets for good measure. I got in first and made my way to the stern while Ben got in and sat in the midsection with the oars. First he would show me how to row until I felt comfortable enough to take the oars myself. In my own thinking, it wouldn't take long at all until I was sufficiently confident to row myself. Maybe I would even row Ben back and go out on my own later in the day.

With a quick shove of his arm, Ben pushed us away from the slip, grabbed an oar in each hand and the blades cut into the water as he pulled, his hands tight on the grips. Then in a fluid motion, he bent down to his waist, pushing his arms out in front of him, and the blades brushed just above the surface of the water. It was one of the most beautiful and graceful things I had ever seen. My knowledge of rowing was next to nothing at that time, but watching him that day in the surf, I knew he had mastered the craft and I was mesmerized by the oars' graceful dance down into and through the water and back up with a delicate turn, returning and commencing the cycle once more. The art of rowing is never done justice by words; one must watch a master at work on the open water to truly appreciate the beauty of rowing.

Ben then began to explain the process of rowing. For the next fifteen minutes, Ben rowed us out in the bay and around, turning, gliding all the while constantly giving little tips and points. He explained that keeping the boat perpendicular to the waves would help to keep it from capsizing. Whenever a he saw any birds, fish or other wildlife, he would point them out with a wonder in his voice which I found humorous. But he was teaching me the craft I had been eager to learn since day one. I fell in love with the *Santiago* that day on the water. The vessel cut so steadily and smoothly through the water and seemed so very proud and free. Before dismissing the idea as ridiculous, for a minute I was even jealous of the boat, cursing my very humanity, but quickly I thought of how the boat's freedom was completely reliant on that very humanity and I felt foolish. The sun was warm on my skin and the occasional spray of cool sea water felt wonderful, and I hadn't even noticed the slip fading away into the distance.

Truth be told, it was everything I had hoped it would be. The people were gone, my worries and memories were pushed and hidden in the back of my mind. I was without a care. I was free and on the open sea, and I realized how glad I was to be with Ben. He was just about the only person who did not, in some unintentional way, remind me of the past or bother me in some other way. We both seemed to leave each other well-enough-alone and we were both very content with that. That day, I realized we had a lot more in common than I had ever realized before. Seeing the way he came alive out on the water, rowing away from the shore and land, it really seemed as thought we were chasing similar destinies.

However, as he continued to row, my frustration began to grow. It looked easy enough; when would he let me try I wondered, and slowly anger began to build because I felt as though I would spend the entire afternoon watching him row. The last thing I wanted was a lesson that involved no hands-on experience for me. But luckily, just as I was nearing my breaking point, Ben suggested we make the switch. Acknowledging the difficulty of the maneuver, we decided it would be easiest, even if slightly counterproductive, for Ben to move to the bow and I from the stern to the middle seat, and after some brief shaky seconds, we came to rest in our new positions. Eagerly, I wrapped my hands around the rough wooden grips of the old oars and eyed the blades for my first attempt.   The blade on the starboard side fell completely into the water alongside the boat while the portside blade barely broke the surface. This caused the former to barely move and the latter to cut quickly through as I brought the grips to my chest. Each oar turned a different angle and the boat made a sharp turn with no forward progress. I was immediately frustrated and angry. Ben had made the process seem so simple and careless, but it was actually incredibly difficult. I wanted this though, badly enough to work for it, so I fought off the anger and tried again. This time the grip in the right hand scraped along the surface of my left hand.

"Damn it!" the frustration spilled out without my realization.

"You all right there, Sam?"

"It's not as easy as you made it look," was my sharp response.

"Well, keep in mind I've been doing it since I was a boy, that's years of practice. My first time, heck, my first couple summers, I was next to worthless. But in time and in practice it'll come."

I knew he meant to help calm my frustration, but his telling me it took him several summers to get better than worthless made me mad. I couldn't believe it would take that long that for me to get the hang of it, but I managed to gather myself and give it another go. This time both oars cut through the water at similar depths and as I brought my hands out to restart the motion, they both stayed above water. I counted it as a moral victory, especially as the boat cut steadily through the water.

"Simple as that," Ben joked. I couldn't find the humor to muster a response.

For the next half hour the boat moved awkwardly through the water. It was entirely due to ineptness of my rowing. Occasionally luck would have it, and I would manage a series of decent strokes, but they were always broken up by periods of struggle and unruly oars. It was truly a bittersweet experience, for I had my first day on the open sea and the freedom involved with that, yet I realized that it would be a much more difficult and longer process to gain the proficiency I longed for. I resigned myself to be satisfied to spend the rest of the time watching Ben as he effortlessly propelled the boat through the sea.

Occasionally small waves would break over the side of the boat.

"Feeling any seasickness?" Ben inquired.

"No, I couldn't feel better," I said with sincerity.

"That's a good sign you were meant to be out here."

Nothing had ever sounded better, confirmation from one whom I considered an expert. It truly was my destiny, my calling. The constant movement of the water and the beautiful shades of blue in the sky intrigued me. I could stare for hours and never get bored. Sometimes I would find myself watching the distant shore, making out places I knew or looking for ospreys' and eagles' nests high in the branches of the old pines. I still got butterflies of excitement every time I saw one of those majestic birds of prey flying overhead. Sitting in the rowboat I leaned back and let the tips of my fingers break the surface of the water. The resistance of the water against the forward force of my hand provided a cool rush of pleasure. Ben and I would go for long periods without a single word and that was perfect. Occasionally Ben would just point, either to a fish surfacing, a bird diving, or another boat in the distance, without a word between us. It was one of those afternoons that on land went so slowly and time came to a halt, but on this day, on the water, it seemed as though we had just gotten started and already it was way past noon. We agreed to do the same thing the following weekend as Ben began to direct the *Santiago* back towards the boathouse.

Without warning a gentle sprinkle began to fall on the water. It lasted less than several minutes but I enjoyed the sight of the drops of rain joining the vast water of the bay. Some droplets fell into Ben's beard and were suspended there by the wiry hair. But before it gained momentum the brief rain was over, and the rest of the way back to the slip was without problem, just the gentle rowing propelling the boat to its destination.

As we neared the house, I could see Pops and Gran sitting together on the back porch in their rocking chairs. We continued on and together they got up hand in hand and walked out to the rock where I had spent the previous summer watching Ben return and they stood there, watching us in, Pops with his arm around Gran's shoulders, while she held firmly to his waist with her head resting on his shoulder. It was a beautiful sight, I must admit, but it sent a wave of terrible loneliness through me. I had nobody to hold, there was no one in the world who would look as completely contented in my arms as Gran looked there in Pop's. I wondered if I would ever know that feeling but quickly pushed out that foolish thought. I didn't need anybody, and even if I had someone like that, it wouldn't be long before they stopped liking me, or realized I was not who they thought I was. Or I would mess up and scare them away. That was a pain I did not want and I determined that I would be alone. Alone was best, no one to hurt you, no one to leave you, no one to lose.

Ben put the oars inside the boat and with a jolt, the *Santiago* was back at the slip. Ben grabbed the slip's edge and pulled the rowboat alongside. I got out, grabbed the oars from him, and put them back in the boathouse. By the time I returned to the slip, Ben had pulled the boat from the water and together we brought it back to where it belonged in the boathouse. The first step in my journey to freedom had begun. It was not quite as I had expected it to be, but I was closer to the end and that was all I needed.

The next week we worked on the landscaping for several old ladies Ben knew from church. The work was mostly weeding, mowing, and planting. It was a lot less labor intensive than the brick work from the previous week, meaning we could start later in the morning and often finished earlier in the afternoon. It was a welcome break to being totally exhausted and covered in cement every day. The work was more relaxing and I was able to observe nature and appreciate it more. During this week, I would come home and be able to spend more time with Pops and Gran. Of course I would still occasionally go off on my own for long stretches of time, but for some reason this week, my nerves and temper were calm. I was thankful for that because it opened up opportunities for some great conversation with Pops.

It began on Monday. All day at work with Ben, I had been so mad with the family I had been born into; outside of Pops and Gran, they seemed worthless. Memories and stories had been boiling up in my mind all day and by the time I finally got home, I was ready to explode, and I walked into the house, right past Pops and Gran without saying hello and went out to the rock and sprawled out.

"You doing all right, Sam?"

I just about fell into the ocean I was so startled. I hadn't heard Pops follow me out and that just made me even more mad, so I finally let the top off and poor Pops was the victim of all my frustrations.

"Yeah, I just hate being a member of a shitty family. You ever get tired of being the only good man in the family?"

As always, as soon as the words left my lips I wished I could do anything to take them back, but the damage was done and they sank into Pops like a dagger. His cheerful old face was suddenly broken into a portrait of grief and pain. At the moment, his eyes looked like Ben's and realizing this, I was very unsettled. Why did I always do this? The few people who cared about me in the entire world were always the victims of my harshness. Pops, although clearly saddened and hurt, remained calm.

"Sammy, there's a lot about our family to be proud of, damn proud of." That was the first time I had ever heard Pops swear, so I knew he was serious. It was hard to believe my family, including myself, were all contemptible and I hated them all. My real dad, Pops' and Gran's son, my mother and I were all worthless. My mom's parents were both dead, but all she ever talked about was how selfish and angry they were. We all seemed to fit the same mold. Pops and Gran were strangely out of place in the family, and it did not make sense. I would give anything to have been born into the countless happy and carefree families I saw all around me. Not only did I hate what had happened to me, I hated that Pops and Gran, who were wonderful people, had to deal with scum like the rest of us.

"I know your father let you down. Well, he let us all down and that hurts, but there are way more Slade men who have done great things. You are the inheritor of a great name, that one person cannot change."

"Yeah, sounds like a good story, but in my experience it's quite the opposite."

"Well I'm sorry it seems that way Sam, I'm real sorry."

"So am I."

"Do you know much about the Civil War, Sam?"

"What the hell does that have to do with anything?"

"Well your great-great-great-grandfather fought in a great battle in that war. You remember the Battle of Gettysburg?"

"Yeah." My interest was rising by the moment. I loved learning about the Civil War. Many days growing up, I had hoped with everything in me that someone of my ancestors had done their part. I always pictured them as great generals, winning major battles. I was listening with everything in me.

"Well the family has been in Maine since before the Revolutionary War. When the Civil War broke out, Isaiah Holt Slade wanted to enlist but his son was sick and he knew the family needed him. But when his son recovered, he enlisted just when they were forming the 20th Maine Volunteer. He was a private."

My eyes must have been glowing. I had gone from feeling horrible to feeling on top of the world. I felt a sense of pride about my name for the first time ever in my life. I am afraid I was even smiling.

I could see Pops' mood improving as well. He was so proud, and I know he wanted me to feel the same way.

"Well, he marched under Chamberlain to Gettysburg. They were the flank of the Army of the Potomac and stationed on Little Round Top. They fought off wave after wave of the Rebel attack and finally ran out of ammunition and with no other options, they charged directly into the Confederate attack. And you know what, Sam? Isaiah Holt Slade put his bayonet on his rifle and charged bravely into the oncoming bullets. He was struck in the chest and bled to death on that hill that day. He died for America, he died for his family, and he died in honor and I'll tell you what, I will never be ashamed to say I am a Slade."

I had no words. Never before had I felt this emotional in a good way. I could not believe it: One of my ancestors had died for what he believed in. I was proud. And then, right at that moment, my father popped into my mind and rage came over me again. How had we gone from such honorable and wholesome people to the shit I called my dad? How does that happen? Pushing those thoughts out of my mind, I pictured the charge of the 20th Maine down Little Round Top that day. I had seen it in my history class and it gave me chills as Chamberlain yelled, "Bayonets!" and they swarmed down into the attack. I knew I had to show that to Pops. Suddenly it seemed a lot more meaningful.

"You know what, Sam. Someday I'll take you to Gettysburg and we can walk the very slope where he died and visit his grave at Gettysburg National Cemetery. Would you like that?"

"I would love that, Pops."

I was so glad he had shared that information with me that day. I still hated my dad and my family, but a small glimmer of hope and a seed of positive energy were planted deep inside me. It would not become evident for a while but for the first time I did not feel like just another person in a long line of failures. I felt like a failure in a long line of great people, which sounds foolish, I know,   but that meant something, there was salvation in that and there was something to be proud of, even if it was long gone.

Ben and I rowed every weekend that summer. No matter what work we did during the week, whether it was brickwork, landscaping, painting or helping him out with some of his carpentry, I always spent the whole week looking forward to Saturday, for the sea was calling and I was learning.   It seemed each time we went out, I performed better than I had the previous outing. The rowing was not so awkward anymore and the motions began to become second nature. Now, I was still a long way off from being comfortable or even good but I was much better than I had been.   Ben   noticed   this   and   by   one midsummer Saturday, he let me row the entire time.

The relationship between Ben and me grew strong that summer but not because of words or getting to know each other. I can say I knew the same things about Ben's past at the end of the summer that I had known at the beginning and he of mine. But for some reason that brought us closer, the acceptance and peace with the unknown allowed us to bond in a way that we both struggled to do with others. That isn't to say I wasn't curious as to what burden Ben was bearing or what tragedy had befallen him, but he didn't dig up my pain so I would leave his alone as well. He would come home from work and have dinner with Pops, Gran and me on occasion at Gran's insistence. Every time after he left, Gran would say, "I love that boy to death, but he seems so incredibly sad. So sad."

It was true, but that was fine by me. I'm sure whenever I left for work she said the same thing to Pops about me, replacing sad with angry. For the most part Pops and Gran and I all got along well that summer, but I did have my occasional meltdown and they were my most common victims. They dealt with so many moods, so much hurt that dripped from my tongue but they never complained and they never offered anything but love in response.

Pops was a man of his word and near the end of the summer, I took off work and he drove me down to Gettysburg. It was a guys' trip, so Gran stayed at home. The night before we left, I showed Pops the movie "Gettysburg." When it came to the charge of the 20th Maine, there were tears in Pops' eyes and when the movie was over we both were silent. The next day, we drove down to Gettysburg and checked into our hotel. Immediately we went to Little Round Top and stood in the very place where we imagined Isaiah Holt Slade had stood, bravely defending the hill. We imagined together Chamberlain being much like Jeff Daniels' portrayal in the movie, nervous yet sure as he had the men fix bayonets and then with passion lead the charge down the slope. We wondered where on the hill Isaiah had fallen. Did he suffer long? It seemed so honorable a way to die, yet a lonely death. I imagined him lying there, mortally wounded, thinking about his family and how they would get along without him. Did he regret his choice to enlist during that moment or did he lie there, proud, knowing his family would be better off when the cause he was fighting for was settled?

So many questions; but I had peace with the unknown. I could fill the blanks in on my own. I wondered if there would ever be anything in my life worth dying for. I knew I had wanted to die plenty of times, but that was always to escape, not to give my life but to take it. I bet it would feel amazing to believe so deeply in something and to be that devoted and sure. I figured I would never know. Pops and I walked together to the great field scattered with grave markers and walked the rows until we came to it. Right there in front of us was the marker. It was such a small and minute memorial to someone who was now so large and important to me.

That trip was the highlight of my summer. It was the longest I had gone in years without exploding or getting incredibly depressed. All of the memories from that journey were happy and I said and did nothing I regretted, a rare outcome at that time in my life. While we were driving home, Pops looked me in the eyes and gave me the best news I had ever heard, "I've been watching you out rowing with Ben and I think you're good enough to where you can take *Santiago* out anytime you want as long as you let me know."

He had said it without emotion, just laid the words right out there for me, but to me it was an emancipation proclamation. Finally, the chains were gone and I could, in Gran's words, "Seize the sea." Whenever I was mad or angry or sick of people I would go out and row. The times when I used to go out among the trees and lie for hours would now be spent rowing around the bay. There was a great freedom and escape in it for me, but I realized my dream was in the clouds and though I could go out and escape, I always would eventually have to return. I was never truly free. In fact, it may have been worse because now I knew what it was like to be free and escape and yet I could not attain that on a permanent basis. This realization came to me the last Saturday of the summer. I had been out on a hot day, the sun beating down, and I had decided to take off my shirt. Sweat dripped down my forehead and into my eyes and I could feel it rolling in beads down my back. I loved every minute of it. The cold spray of the sea felt that much more wonderful on my hot skin and I loved the feeling of doing hard work.

I was quite a way out from any other boats and land and was relishing the moment. But then it hit me, it would not last. I had been so emotionally high up to that point and felt as though I could take on the world but suddenly it all crashed into nothing. I smacked the oar on the water, my head fell into my hands, and without warning, I began to sob. I wept out there on the sea, uncontrollably, and it seemed as though I would never be able to escape it. I felt helpless. I cried and cried and wasn't ashamed because not a soul was around. Momentarily I thought about just rowing nonstop out into the vast sea, to where even the islands could not be seen and there wasn't a boat in sight and then just rowing until I could row no more. I thought I would just lie there until I died. But I was afraid, I did not know what came after death, but I knew I deserved some kind of hell. I finally collected myself, replaced the oars in the locks and began rowing back towards the shore.

FIVE

Time began to rush by and before I knew it, my senior year was upon me. I did very well that year, largely due to the fact I had chosen not to make any friends and therefore had nothing better to do with my time than actually concentrate and focus in school. I enjoyed reading although no one in the world was aware of it, except perhaps Pops and Gran. We had talked on occasion about my post-high school plans and the general consensus was that I could attend a college of my choice. I had no burning desire to go to college, but at the same time I had no appealing alternatives so I figured, why not? Pops and Gran would pay for it if I did decide to go.

Thus began the search for the right school. Colleges in 49 states were immediately ruled out as I decided to stay in Maine and within reasonable distance of home, *Santiago* and the sea. I looked at school after school, but my heart was set on Bowdoin College in Brunswick. My bias towards Bowdoin in large part had to do with the fact it was the school of Chamberlain, the commander of the 20th Maine, as well as of my old friends, Nathaniel Hawthorne and Henry Wadsworth Longfellow, authors of the antiquarian books in my room. Pops, Gran and I made a visit, I applied, and I found out not long thereafter that I had been accepted. My plan was to major in English Literature. I had no idea what I would do with that degree, but it was one subject I enjoyed. The only problem was that my secret obsession with books and reading would be out.

Senior year flew by, and I succeeded in graduating with honors as well as in not making a single real friend throughout my entire high school experience. I remained close to Ben throughout the rest of my days in high school, and worked with him doing odd jobs as usual whenever we had a chance. I was still consumed with anger and had a quick temper, but I was improving and actually had many fond memories of my times with Pops and Gran. There was a part in me that would be sad to leave them behind for college, but I knew I needed a change and needed to get out. Pops and Gran threw a little graduation party for me. The only guest was Ben, so I guess I could say that all my friends were there. We had clam chowder and toasted English muffin bread, my favorite. Then we all went out to the porch for presents. The first was from Pops and Gran. She handed me a brown paper-wrapped package with tears welling in her eyes. I carefully tore the paper off. A magnificent album lay beneath.

"Go ahead take a look inside," Pops said, gleaming

I opened the front cover and the title page read, "The Slade Family History," along the top. Centered on the page was an old photograph of Pops' father in his World War II Navy blues. Underneath was written, "A Proud Tradition of Patriotism, Sacrifice, and Love." I flipped through the pages and was quickly lost in time.

The album began with Isaiah Holt Slade's father, Samuel Slade, and told his story, of how he was a sawmill hand in Maine. He married Deborah Holt in the 1820's and Isaiah Holt Slade, their only child to survive to adulthood, was born in 1827. It gave account of Isaiah's story and all the Slades from him until Pops. Wherever possible, there were pictures and other little bits of family history. I flipped from person to person, reading amazing stories of hard work, dedication to family and a lot of sacrifice. Eager to see what came after Pops, I found that my father had been purposely omitted and that the album skipped straight to me. There were baby pictures and some other pictures interspersed through the creative writing Gran had done to make my story fit the theme of the album. The last page was a picture of Pops, Gran and me and they had written, "…the rest is yours to write…"

I loved the album and the joy of the moment helped keep me from getting angry that of all those great Slades, I was born to the only one who was a failure and omitted from the album. Pushing those thoughts from my mind, I thanked Pops and Gran for the album. They must have worked hard on it for months and done it in such secrecy, I had no idea. But then I thought of how much time I was spending out on the sea in the rowboat and realized that they would have had plenty of time to work on it. Next Ben handed me an envelope and inside there was a picture of a Jeep.

"It's for you," he explained. "I bought it and have been working on it to get it all tuned up and in condition. That way you can get to and from school. You know those weekends when you want to just come home and row."

"Thank you so much!" I exclaimed with obvious excitement.

We went around front. He had driven it to the house and in the excitement of the day, I had not even noticed it when he arrived. He showed off the work he had done. It was a Wrangler, about ten years old, but he had done great work with it. He started it up and I drove him and Pops for a test drive while Gran began dinner. For a moment I was emotional, although as usual I never let it show. Driving with Pops and Ben, I realized that soon my surroundings, my friends, and my comfort zone would all be gone. It worried me how it would go, being around so many people and, worst of all, having a roommate. That was something I was not excited about at all and, honestly, was afraid of, even dreading. Realizing that soon I would be looking back and wishing I had more moments like the one I was in, I focused on the present and conversation with Ben and Pops. We stayed up late into the night laughing and just enjoying each other's company, a rare jewel of a time for someone with my temperament and one I have never forgotten.

That summer was much like the previous one and my time was spent toiling away with Ben on various jobs, whatever work people needed to have done. The work ranged from extremely hard to pleasant and it was nice to spend the time with Ben. Something in me also forced me to spend more time with Pops and Gran, and it seemed that unless something triggered me, I was a lot better at controlling my emotions. This was the longest I had ever gone without making Gran cry. It was a truly happy summer. On Saturdays, I would be out on the sea in the *Santiago,* rowing from morning until dinner. We continued to go to church every Sunday. It didn't interest me much. I enjoyed people-watching and some of the songs, but I could do without the preaching. It just made me feel guilty. Every Sunday, without fail, Ben would bring the old widow he had always helped; she was even more feeble and had even more difficulty getting about. For me, the sea was my church, my sanctuary, my holy place. For me, going out and spending a day rowing was almost like worship. There was something to the escape that made it feel like more than a physical experience. I could not imagine my life without it, but I knew that soon it would not be that available to me. Soon I would spend Saturdays studying or on the ponds around Bowdoin in the Brunswick Lakes region.

Towards the end of summer, Pops, Gran and I went shopping and got everything we thought I would need for school and I packed up what few belongings I had in my new Jeep. I made sure I had my family album and some of my favorite old books, then Pops and Gran followed behind me to Brunswick and helped me move into school. We finished unpacking and they took me out to dinner. Sitting there, eating a lobster roll and clam chowder, I got extremely angry. I was mad I had to grow up, I was mad I was at school, I was mad I would be in a new place.

Finally, in my life things had seemed to be going well and I was happy and now it would all change and I had no control over it. Cursing my situation, I turned inward and cold toward Pops and Gran for the rest of the night and barely even said goodbye after dinner. I drove back to my dorm and enjoyed the only night I would have without a roommate, angry and punching my pillow.

I woke up early the next morning, disheartened that I would not have Pops and Gran to join me for a morning cup of coffee. I thought of their drive back home after dropping me off the day before. I knew they were sad to leave me and I knew they loved me but something deep inside me wanted them to be glad to drop me off, relieved I would no longer be with them. No matter how hard I tried, though, they could not be forced to hate me in my head and then it made me loathe myself for how I treated them. To escape my tormenting thoughts, I got dressed, grabbed a book from my dresser and walked out of the room, through the hall, down the stairs and out into the chilly morning air.

The chill caught me and my body tightened in a shake trying to keep warm. Suddenly all my thoughts scattered to clear the way for the most important thought of the day: coffee. I walked the campus looking for a place to get some, but then I remembered a Dunkin' Donuts we had passed the day before. I set my path and my heart and had visions of steam rising from a fresh brewed cup. Two birds gawked noisily at each other up on the power lines across the road. I felt sorry for them that they could not drink coffee and immediately laughed at the foolishness of such a thought. Ahead I could see the Dunkin' Donuts and an old man with a beard even larger than Ben's smoking as he leaned against his truck in the parking lot. He greeted me as I walked past him and into the shelter of the store. I was oblivious to any details of the interior and who was there or what was being consumed. I walked up to the counter, ordered a large coffee with cream and a shot of French vanilla and waited as I watched the man, who could be no older than myself, make the coffee and wish me a pleasant morning. I took a sip and immediately burnt my tongue. Damn it, I hated when I did that, but it was good coffee so I accepted the burned tongue as a price to pay.

I turned to find a place to drink my java and read. At one table, a group of jolly old men sat, drinking coffee and reminiscing. The man who had been smoking in the parking lot was now sitting with them, gulping the last of his coffee. Past them, a younger man in a suit and tie sat staring intently at his laptop screen. He seemed so odd and out of place to me as I had only seen men in suits at church or funerals. Looking past him, in the far corner, was a young woman who had to be about my age. She was beautiful, yet simple. She sat
with her legs crossed, in khaki pants.Her slender torso was hidden in a soft sky-blue hoodie, partially zipped, concealing a black t-shirt. She wore a silver necklace with some medallion around her neck and earrings which were diamonds or glass imitations. In her right hand she held a novel. I squinted to make out the title, but I couldn't and I realized it probably looked as though I was standing there, starring at her, so I quickly found a seat at a table two away from hers. From there I took a sip of my coffee. I could read the title clearly now. It was French, *Le Comte de Monte-Cristo*. I do not speak French but felt it was safe to assume that she was reading *The Count of Monte Cristo*. I liked her immediately. I fought it momentarily, but I couldn't help it. I had already made enough assumptions about her to fall helplessly in love.

There was no state in the world I hated more than being in love. My first assumption was that she had to be my age or near it. My second, possibly immense, assumption was that she was smart. She had to be to be reading a classic like that in French. I only liked intelligent girls. In fact, a great pet peeve of mine was ignorant or ditzy girls. After

82

these wild assumptions, I made a wish: I wished she was a student a Bowdoin. She had not looked up once since I had laid eyes on her. I had opened my book and was sitting so it looked as though I were reading if anyone looked, when in all reality, I was taking her in. Occasionally to help shield the truth, I would glance out the window or look all around the Dunkin' Donuts.

Her hair looked as though it was originally a dark brunette but had been dyed blonde, which formed a mixture of a dark blonde and light brunette. She had thin eyebrows and small eyes. I could not decide if they were green or blue, but I decided they were beautiful. Her nose was prominent but seemed to fit her face perfectly. Her lips were full and held tight as though she was reading a tense portion of her book. As I sat there wondering who she was, what she did or how to get to know her, I did not notice a single customer come or go, I didn't even realize the group of old men had gone or that a another young woman was now sitting with the professional man. I hated myself for already cultivating such feelings towards this mystery girl. It was only my first day of college and classes hadn't even started. I felt strongly that I shouldn't nurture feelings like this; it was against everything I had tried to become.

I had forgotten to turn the pages in my book. My gaze turned to the window and I watched families of students, walking around the campus and moving in. Every time I saw a new student with two parents, I hated them. I was sure they weren't thankful for what they had and a tinge of jealousy rose in me.

However, my attention was quickly diverted back to the girl as she put her book down on the table. She took the last sip of her drink, gathered her purse and then stood up to leave. My seat was in the path from where she was seated to the trash can and door. Immediately I stared down at my book. As she walked by, it took all my will power not to look up and make eye contact. With a light noise, her cup fell to the ground right next to my table. "Pick it up, pick it up, Sam," I said to myself over and over again in my head. It was my break, my big chance to at least make initial contact. But my body froze and my hand lifted just to turn a page in my book. Before I knew it, the opportunity passed and she was walking out the door. I looked up and watched her cross the street and walk onto the Bowdoin campus. Disappointed with myself for my lack of action, I sat momentarily wallowing in my own emotions, and then I decided to move on. I walked out the door and through the busy morning campus. Entering the library, I made my first check out as a college student, Victor Hugo's *The Hunchback of Notre-Dame*. I returned to my room and was glad to find that my roommate was yet to arrive.

I actually had begun to wonder if my roommate would show and I was fighting the urge to get excited that maybe at the last minute he had decided not to go to college. It was reminiscent of days in high school spent trying to keep from getting hopes up about the possibility of a snow day. It was early evening when those hopes were dashed and my peace and solitude were disturbed by the sound of a key in the door; damn it, he was there. He walked through the door, tall, about 6 feet, 3 inches yet extremely lanky, probably 150 pounds. His hair was buzzed and he had on long baggy shorts and a shirt with caricatures of vampires. He walked right up to me.

"You must be Sam?" and then before I could respond, "I'm D, well, Dale, but everyone calls me D. I'm a huge vampire and zombie fan. I hope that's all right."

What? I wasn't quite sure if I would mind or not, not exactly sure what being a huge vampire and zombie fan entailed. He began to unload his masses of computer equipment and clothes. Not eager to help and with a strong desire to get out of the way, while he was on one of his trips to his car, I walked out into the breezy pre-dusk. To be completely honest, I had not been able to get the girl from the coffee shop off of my mind all day. I was determined to get to know her, yet scared and certain that it would end horribly. I walked around campus, occasionally taking a break and sitting on a bench, people watching, but mostly just biding my time until I felt I could go back to the room and not have to worry about being asked to help my roommate.

Now, either luck does not exist or I have none, because I waited for the sun to set, figuring it'd be safe to return. When I walked through the door I realized I was quite wrong, the only thing he had brought in was a massive PC set up which he sat behind commanding some sort of game. He took off his headset, "Great, man, now you can help me unpack!" What the hell? I was so pissed. Are you kidding me? Why in the world would he wait for me?

"Are you serious?"

"Yeah, sure." D looked at me dumbfounded as though he couldn't believe I wasn't eagerly coming back for the sole purpose of helping him unpack his car.

"I was waiting for you, man," he said with a laugh, the words striking every wrong chord in me.

Even though all I wanted to do was to walk out, I angrily agreed and half an hour later, lugging boxes up the stairs, we were done. During the entire process, I did my best to make it clear I was not pleased to be helping him, and that it was in fact the complete opposite,

but the effort seemed lost on D. I got in bed and closed my eyes while he, without regard to the noise, unpacked between
games on his PC. That night I really hated D, but as time went on, I actually grew to like him. We never spent much time together; he was always playing his games or watching some zombie movie, but that was perfect as far as I was concerned. I realized that, maybe like me, he was trying to escape this world, find another place he could be at peace. To me, we had a lot in common and as he went into his fantasy world of games, I spent as much time out of the room and away from people.

The next morning I once again woke up early. D was in bed, still in his jean shorts and boots from the day before. I got ready and grabbed *The Hunchback of Notre-Dame* on my way out the door, headed to Dunkin'. I was excited at the possibilities that might lie ahead in the day. Maybe today was the day to finally meet my mystery woman. I was unaware of the weather, and the anger from yesterday had melted away into a happy anticipation. I walked through the doors and the same group of old men was enjoying their cups. I looked around frantically for my mystery lady to no avail. Ordering my drink, I continued to look over my shoulder, hoping that she would come through the door at any moment. I found a seat in the corner near where she sat the day before, from where I could easily watch the entire store and also look out the window to keep an eye out. Why would I expect her to be here anyway? How dumb was I, and how could I let myself be controlled and fall for someone I have not met but have only seen? In the midst of my personal struggling, I picked up my book and realized I really had no interest in reading it; I only wanted her to see me reading it. I held it there and thought to myself; why did I wake up so early for this? What an idiot!

My hope was fading and it was going fast. I resolved to sit there; the only good thing I could think of was at least I got a nice cup of coffee out of it. For an hour and a half I sat, constantly looking around. Anyone who saw me no doubt thought I was either hiding from someone, running from the police, or just plain paranoid. Every time a car pulled up, a jump of hope would rise within me only to be shattered when anyone but my mystery woman stepped out the door. I realized I was wasting my time and, it being the first day of class, I needed to make sure I was not late to my eleven o'clock "Intro to English Literature" class. Slowly, I stood up and walked to the trashcan like a prisoner to the gallows. Turning towards the door, my gaze dropped to the floor. I was so disappointed. It was not that she did not show, but that I had let something work me up this much. That really bugged me. It was stupid and I would not let it happen again. I walked through the door and the sun was warm on my face.

Walking to the crosswalk, a car pulled in right in front of me. I could not believe it: Out stepped the girl. A Maine license plate: That was a good sign, maybe she was local. Her beauty once more cast a spell on me as she got out of her car and walked in. Why was the world so cruel? I had spent an hour and a half waiting and in a matter of seconds I had missed my opportunity? Everything I had cast off and all the feelings rushed back and I knew I would never have peace until I talked to her. But today wasn't the day; the thought of it twisted my stomach and made my heart race. Quickly I crossed the street and headed back to the room.

That night Ben called me. All I could picture when I was talking to him was the hair on his mustache moving up and down with the motion of his words. He asked about school and how the first day of class went. He said he had accepted an invite to Gran's and Pops' house for dinner every day since I had left, and that he could tell they really missed me. Being missed was a new experience for me. I had been taken away from my birth mom and she had not once called, written or made any attempt to see how I was. I wasn't missed by her. My real father -- who the hell knew where he was? But wherever he was, I doubted I would ever cross his mind. How could anyone like me enough to miss me? I did not even like myself that much. I would be perfectly content to be dead and not have to deal with my endless thoughts and being with myself. I also felt bad because Gran and Pops missed me, apparently a lot, and I didn't really miss them that much. Don't get me wrong, I did miss them, but it did not cause me to get sad or affect any part of my daily routine. I was glad Ben had called and I thought about asking about the mystery girl but kept convincing myself not to until he finally broke the ice.

"So, any girls catch your eye?"

"Well..." my silence gave it away.

"That's the response of someone knocked off their feet! Please fill me in!"

I went on to explain about the Dunkin' Donuts girl. I was spilling my feelings as I never had before and Ben listened quietly and occasionally would throw in an agreeing "uh huh" or "yeah". When I came to the end of my rambling, I laid it out. "I don't know what to do, it's a horrible feeling, I wished I had never seen her."

It surprised me how honest and open I was. I guess I felt safe with Ben and the distance and the fact we were speaking on the telephone made me feel that much more secure.

"It's a wonderful feeling, isn't it?" came his reply, "I haven't felt that way in years, and I never will again."

What the hell does that mean? What does that have to do with anything?

"But let me just say back in the day I had a little bit of experience."

OK, now you're talking, Ben. Fill me in, was what I thought, but I only uttered, "OK?"

"I know it'll be hard and you may look like a fool, but you have to be bold and take the chance or you will only regret it and wonder what may have been if you had been so bold as to just step out and open yourself up."

"But how?"

"Now there's the difficult part!"

"No joke." My voice was dull and serious.

"I guess my only advice is to take the chance."

As much as I would have thought differently, that advice actually was encouraging to me. He was right. I would never know what could have been if I didn't do what was in my power to do, to open up the opportunity to it. I had to take this risk, and I always had my escape, the sea. I figured things were tilted in my favor. I had seen her twice, but to my knowledge she had only seen me once, if that. So I figured it was still early enough to initiate conversation without looking creepy. But I told myself if I passed up one more opportunity I would have to just tuck tail and face the fact that I was too afraid and move on. This was really to motivate myself. Deep down inside I think I knew I would try until it was completely impossible, but I needed the motivation. I went to bed to the sound of zombies being destroyed, with confidence for the next day. While I was lying there, daydreaming before sweet sleep took over, I pictured myself starting a conversation with her that ended in rejection and immediately driving to the coast, getting in my boat and rowing, rowing until I could not see shore, rowing with a big beard like Ben's. Rowing away from everything and being free.

Waking up the next morning early as usual, I got ready for the day and snuck out of the room without D noticing. Briskly I began to walk to Dunkin', but I decided to stay casual and calm. Confidence was the key. When Dunkin' came into sight, I looked throughout the parking lot for her car, but it was nowhere in sight. OK, that's fine, stay calm. When the time is right, the time is right. Of course, I began to look all down both directions of the street for her car to come speeding by. Yet there was no luck. I reached the door and could see in the windows; no mystery woman. Trying hard to cover my disappointment I went to the counter and ordered my usual. I sat down and drank my coffee, but decided not to wait, I was too disappointed. When I had finished the last sip I got up and left. Oh well, I tried.

I had another early class, but there was still time to waste before it began. I opted not to return to the room.   D and I were getting along fine, but I preferred to spend most of my time alone. I don't think it bothered him that I was never there, because he could play his games without his headset on. I had started to read *The Hunchback* even though I knew my motives for buying it had been a little obscure. I found a nice bench outside the building where my class was to be held and decided to read until class began.

"What do you think of the book?"

My heart froze, it was a sweet voice, but one I did not recognize. Slowly looking up from the pages, I saw her standing there. This was impossible. It was too easy. I could not believe that not only was it outside of Dunkin', but she had initiated the conversation. In hindsight, I realize that I never would have garnered the guts to strike up a conversation. Immediately any confidence that I thought I had completely disappeared. My heart suddenly was beating as if I had just finished a strenuous run.

"Well, I'm not very far into it, but so far I like it," was my response. Weak, that's all you could mutter? I immediately felt as though she would assume I was dumb. I liked it? Yeah, that's real deep. My one chance and I blew it. My face felt flushed and I was sure I must have looked like a fool.

"Well, it's better in French," she said with a wink and smile. Never before in my life had a girl winked at me -- well, other than the elderly ladies at church who were friends with Gran. I was in love. I was determined I would do anything for her and I didn't even know her name.

"Well, I wouldn't know, I struggle enough with English," I said with a slight laugh. Is that your attempt at a joke? Real funny guy huh? I felt the hole I was digging sink deeper and deeper.

"Tell me about it."

I couldn't believe that I was actually having a conversation with her. There she was, standing in front of me, with those deep blue jeans, a bright yellow shirt contrasting with her tan skin. Her hair was pulled back in a messy ponytail and a strand ran down her check. She seemed so joyful and happy. Suddenly the glee of the moment was lost. This was too good to be true. She couldn't be enjoying this and even if she was, it would only a matter of time until I ruined it. It wouldn't last. I told myself, "Don't enjoy it or it will only torment you later."

But then Ben's advice burst through the cloud of doubt, "Take the chance." He was right, I had to take the chance. "My name's Sam, by the way," I reached out my hand to hers. "

Sarah," she accepted my hand. "It's nice to meet you, Sam."

She said my name. Chills ran down my spine. Never before had I been so enamored by someone. But now I understood it. There was a brutal tug of war going on within me, fighting between letting myself completely lose it for this girl and remaining the same withdrawn Sam. But every single time I hesitated, Ben's beard popped into my mind, "Take a chance."

"Mind if I join you?"

"Be my guest. You waiting on a class?"

"Yup, my "Intro to Philosophy" class is in fifteen minutes, so I need to kill some time."

"Yeah, I'm waiting on my "World Civ" class."

I was disappointed we weren't in the same class, yet glad that we were currently talking, so I really felt as though I could not complain. As we continued to talk, a stream of students slowly made their way into the building. I was glad they saw us sitting out there and talking. So many times in life, I had been the jealous one looking at a beautiful girl talking to a guy and now the tables were turned. I found out Sarah was from Rockland, Maine, a town just about 7 miles south of Camden. My mind ran with that, I fought against picturing weekend trips home together. I was sure I was reading more into everything than she was but I couldn't help it. She was a philosophy major but wasn't sure what she was going to do with that. She was fluent in French and loved to read. That was all I needed to hear, she had looks, smarts and personality. When we parted ways, I knew I should plan a time to see her again but I was afraid and so we went to class without any plans. Class was a mixture of being in bliss and being furious with myself for not setting plans. I hoped I would see her again, and hated how timid I was. After a day full of classes, I went to the room and read until D got back. I decided to accept his invite to watch one of his favorite movies. I thought about calling Ben and getting advice, but I was hesitant and it was more convenient to just go to bed after the movie. But lying in bed, I couldn't sleep, with the mix of excitement and fear that was welling up inside. I decided to call Pops and Gran. Gran answered and was thrilled I called. She insisted that I hadn't waked her up, but I knew that wasn't the case since it was almost 11 o'clock. We talked for a while about class and how things were with D and then Pops got on. We didn't talk long but it was nice and a good talk. I was glad I had called and then I fell asleep.

The next morning I woke up and looked at the alarm clock. Damn it! I freaked out. I had slept about half an hour past when I was planning on waking up. I was planning on hitting up Dunkin' again before class. I was so frustrated and mad, I hopped out of bed and quickly got dressed. I felt miserable and on the brink of tears. I just wanted to scream. I walked out of the door, but was too flustered to visit Dunkin'. I would not be able to make myself look or sound good if I ran into Sarah now. I walked around for a little while and was too angry to even think straight. I went back to the room, and got back in bed. It felt uncomfortable, but I didn't care. I lay there and squeezed my pillow trying to relieve the stress.

Before I knew it, I was waking up again. Luckily it was just in time for class. I have to admit, I felt much better than the first time I woke up for the day. I still was frustrated but not nearly as badly as I had been. It was Thursday and the way classes were scheduled, I hoped to meet Sarah in front of the building once more the next day, Friday. I wasn't really ever fully there in class, mostly zoned out thinking of the next day or being nostalgic about the summer. I called Ben after class as I walked back to the dorm and shared with him how the events unfolded. He seemed enthusiastic and excited for me. It was funny how he seemed to be pulling for me; what did he stand to gain from this? I wasn't sure but I didn't mind. It was nice to have a fan and a supporter. But a fear slowly began to build in me. What would Ben think if I screwed it up? How would he take it if I scared her off forever? Not only would I be disappointed, he would be, too. That tore me apart, I hated it when the feelings and emotions of other people rested on me. That was a responsibility I never wanted, and because of that, I decided to not tell Pops and Gran about Sarah for now. Ben's advice was to ask her out for coffee since I knew we both enjoyed it. That I couldn't argue with and as nervous as it made me, I decided next time I saw her, no matter what, I would ask her.

I figured I would arrive for class about fifteen minutes early and wait for her to show, hopefully early, but if not, I would just wait as long as possible. As luck would have it, as I approached I saw that she

94

was sitting there on a bench. I was so excited my heart began to beat rapidly. I made the assumption she had come early to run into me again, and I think I was right. She looked up and smiled a really big smile which I eagerly returned. She cleared her backpack off the bench, which I took as an invitation to sit down next to her. We ran through pleasantries and I put off asking her out as long as possible, but finally as time was running short, I knew I had to ask.

"You got any plans this weekend?" Suddenly I was short of breath.

"Well, no big plans, I'll just be around, I guess."

"I was thinking, if you wanted to, um, go out with me, maybe Saturday night? I was thinking we could get coffee or something, if you want to." Right away, I regretted my wording entirely. The words echoed idiotically in my mind. They were barely literate. I definitely made it clear, only if she wanted to.

But her smile put me at ease, "I would love to!"

SIX

This would be my first official date. I had often wished I could be in love, to have someone to trust completely and someone who trusted me, someone I could confide in and who would understand and not worry about the past but would just build a future together with me. Well, this seemed like my first chance at that and the very prospect of it was amazing to me. I wanted to make sure my first date with Sarah was something she would remember and I wanted to treat her right. Things seemed to be going so well, and I didn't think about escaping out to sea nearly as often and it made being at school actually not half bad.

I picked Sarah up for our date at her dorm. She came through the doors and looked beautiful. Her hair was done up and she seemed so happy with that smile I was falling for. Looking at her, I could not believe someone that beautiful was about to go out and spend the evening with me. Next to her, I felt like a bum, me with my wrinkled polo shirt and my jeans that were loose from too many wears without washing and her with her silky shirt with high cut sleeves and her black pants. I was careful to open the door to her building for her as we left, and when we got to my car, I opened and closed the door for her, just as I always had imagined I would. Walking around the car to get in, I couldn't help but smile.

To avoid an awkward silence, I struck up a conversation about the trivialities of the week and made small talk about classes. I decided to take her to a local independent coffee shop I had tested out the day before. It was quaint little place, but it had the perfect atmosphere to relax in over a great cup. It was a quick drive and, once again, I made sure to open the door for Sarah, at which point, she put her hand on my upper arm and thanked me. Could this really be happening? It was wonderful and I wanted to make sure I didn't screw it up. She walked up to the counter and stood staring at the order board.   Time   seemed suspended as I gazed at her looking intently up at the menu. She ordered a white chocolate mocha and I quickly followed with the largest coffee they had. As I paid, Sarah thanked me and we made our way to the corner table.

I took a sip of my coffee and just stared into her eyes and smiled. This was a contented feeling I had not known. But suddenly, fear struck its awful feeling into my soul. What if she asks about my past? What if she questions me about growing up? Oh no, this was awful. I was almost paralyzed by fear. You can't ruin this, don't let it happen, say something, anything.

"How's your white chocolate mocha?" Yeah, real deep genius. But it didn't focus on the past, so it passed.

"It's delicious, a little hot, but delightful," she continued, "would you like to try it?"

"Sure, want to try my coffee?"

"No, thanks, I'm still learning to like that coffee taste -- it takes a lot of cream and sugar and flavor for me."

I took a sip of her white mocha."Well, now I won't even like my coffee after trying this!"

Whew, she laughed. There is always a moment of suspense between when I try to be funny, and when I find out whether what I said had the intended effect. I did not at all consider myself to be a funny person, but I had called Ben for advice before the date, and he told me girls love a guy that can make them laugh. Of course, this knowledge was a blessing and curse because now I would either make her laugh or think I am a completely humorless idiot, probably the latter.

But it did break the ice and immediately the conversation began flowing. She asked me what it was like back home and I could deal with the recent past, but not digging up anything deeper. I shared all about Pops and Gran, rowing out on the sea, nature, reading, and working with Ben and I had to throw in Gran's clam chowder. I actually felt happy talking about these things. It made me a little nostalgic and I actually missed them briefly. She seemed delighted by all the things I had to say. She did ask once though, "How come you live with your grandparents?" Anger boiled inside me. Why, why did she have to go there? A war ensued within my psyche, and it must have been obvious to her that I was tormented by the question because she quickly withdrew, "I'm sorry, Sam, that's none of my business. Things do seem really great with your Pops and Gran." She reached out and put her hand on my arm and looked deep into my eyes. It was clear she meant what she said. She didn't need to know. I was so used to people prying for answers, wanting to be nosey and know everything and then putting up some facade of caring. But Sarah was genuine; she cared enough to know I didn't want her to care. At least that is the way I read it.

The conversation then carried on without a second thought. I turned the questions to her and I loved hearing about her summer, about what seemed to be a great family and siblings. Normally, when I hear about other people's great families, I get jealous and just shut them off. But I was glad to hear how great Sarah's family seemed to be and how happy it made her. She was such a joyful person and her bubbly personality seemed to rub off on me. I realized I couldn't help but feel more positive around her. She seemed to respond to me, too; she listened and always commented about what I said. It was wonderful to discover that we had a lot in common, that we both loved the outdoors, reading, trying new things and adventure. She made me promise her to take her out in *Santiago* sometime. It was funny how I used to row to escape from everything and get away and was now thrilled at the prospect of taking someone out with me.

We talked for hours on end and were still there when it was closing time. There was never a delay or pause in the conversation, we just learned about each other, shared stories and laughed. I made a couple of attempts at humor and she ate it up. She had a loud burst of a laugh which the first couple of times caught me off guard, but I began to long for it. We walked out and she grabbed my arm as I walked her to the passenger side door. These feelings were all so new to me and I could not believe it. It was the reassurance I needed to confirm that it had gone as well as I thought it had. We drove back and I walked her to her dorm. She turned and gave me a great big hug and before pulling away, she reached up and kissed my cheek.

"I had a great time tonight, Sam. Let's do it again soon!"

"Good night, Sarah," I smiled as she turned before disappearing into her dorm.

Yes! That had gone way better than my wildest dreams. I immediately called Ben. He picked up after one ring and I talked a thousand words a minute as he listened and shared in my excitement. He told me he was proud and to keep him updated. I felt as though I were living someone else's life. Things could not be going this well for me. They never did. That night as I lay in bed, with a smile on my face, I hoped more than anything I would die that night in my sleep. I would die utterly happy, the happiest I had been in years and I would die before I would be able to ruin all the great things that seemed to be going for me and I would never know hurt, pain or anger again.

At Ben's urging I resisted the longing to call her the next day, but come Monday, I went to class extra early and sure enough not long after I got to "our bench" she came smiling up. We talked and planned to go out that night. We both had to study -- well she did -- and I said I did, so we planned to meet at the library.

I had a wonderful time. We were there for several hours and most of them were spent joking with each other and laughing. I really enjoyed my time with her. Actually, I was thinking about it while we were talking and I decided I would share about her with Pops and Gran. I was daydreaming of her coming home and visiting them with me and taking long rides out in the boat. I was in paradise. She was studying for her math Gen Ed, and I spent most of the time reading short stories for my lit class. It was ideal. I would even read aloud to her because I did once, completely joking, and she loved it and kept asking me to read more excerpts to her. Sometimes while she was studying, I would find myself just staring at her. I loved watching her so intently working on something. She would be "in the zone" and not even notice anything going on around her. I would fight the urge to distract her for a while and then give in, always leading to nice breaks from work. She valued education very much and was one of the best students I had ever met. From what I could tell she worked really hard for her grades. It made me almost feel guilty because I didn't feel like I had to try very hard to do well enough. But she did excellently and it was inspiring.

The remainder of the week we spent time together every single day, whether it was a moment before class, a meal, or coffee at night. We got really close really fast. I knew all of her dreams and aspirations for life and she knew not to bring up the past and was fine with that. I found myself calling Ben almost every day to update him and let him know how things were going. After Friday night when I had called him three times and he listened to me rant on and on about how awesome Sarah was, he threw a bit of caution my way, "That's awesome about Sarah, and I'm really glad things are going so well, but make sure you don't take things too fast, Sam. I just know in my experience, it always was better on a slower pace."

"What?! What are you talking about, Ben? Don't you want me to be happy?" I immediately exploded.

"Calm down, Sam, I'm really happy for you," he explained before I interrupted.

"Well, then don't mess with my mind."

After that he just completely changed the subject, which was smart on his part. As good a friend as he had been, I would have completely cut him out of my life. I was so consumed with Sarah, I would do anything to make it work. He knew me well enough to know that the best thing to do was let it be. We talked a little while longer and I was clearly agitated, but it saved things and the next time we talked it was as though the fight had never happened.

Pops and Gran were frustrating, too. Whenever I shared something about Sarah with them, they would always respond with, "That's nice," or something else trivial like that. They never had the enthusiasm I wanted from them; they never seemed truly excited and it made me mad. So, slowly I called them less and less. I guess I was slowly pulling away from all of them as I was going toward Sarah. It was easy for me to do, though, because she was there and around and it was easier to ignore the other people because they weren't there.

Things really snowballed the next week. We started the week out the same way as the previous week except that we were together all the time. I never knew I could spend so much time with anyone, especially without getting mad at them or doing something stupid to ruin it. Of course, I got more and more confident the more time we spent together, but I also got more and more scared. Every moment we weren't together I was worried she would find someone new. My mind was constantly plagued with thoughts of where she might be and who she might be with. She talked of her "other friends" and she spent time with them. I was always very jealous of these friends, and Sarah never afforded me the opportunity to meet them. This bugged me to no end and my curiosity ran rampant, but I loved our relationship and so I put up with it. The nights she was with her "other friends," I would spend fuming in the room, but it was worth it because the nights we spent together were so good. Well, as the week drew to end, Sarah informed me that her roommate was going home for the weekend and she wanted me to come over Friday night and watch a movie with her. Before she even finished asking my response was resounding within me, yes, yes, yes, yes!

This would be my first visit to her place and I had been very afraid that she would ask her "other friends" to hang out, so the double relief led to extra anticipation. The thing was, I had completely stopped fighting against getting my hopes up. It was too late for that. They were high on a pedestal and seemed to get higher every day. Everything was going perfectly, according to plan, until Friday around 11. Something that should have made me incredibly happy ruined the entire day. A phone call.

"Hello?"

"Sam, it's Gran. Pops and I are at Bowdoin, we decided to surprise you!"

"What?!" was my clearly agitated response.

"Is everything ok, Sam?" was her sweet and sincere reply.

"What are you guys doing?"

"We wanted to see you, so we thought we'd drive up for the day and take you out to eat, and maybe some of your friends, like that nice girl you talk about. We just miss you, Sam."

"You think I don't make plans? What do you think I do, sit around all day, waiting for you to call?"

Before I could finish my rant, Gran interrupted. "We're sorry, Sam, we were just being selfish. We didn't want to bother you, we should have called ahead. Please don't be mad at us. We're sorry."

I was as angry as I had been in a while, but not mainly at them. I was furious at myself that I was allowing this to bother me. I knew I should be happy and I was actually thrilled that they missed and wanted to see me, but the day was all wrong, any day but today. How could I treat them so shabbily? I didn't know, and it made me so mad, but in my anger it just got worse and worse.

"I'm sorry, Gran. It's just a bad day. Any day but today."

"We love you, Sam. We care about you very much. We're here anytime."

"I know Gran... I... I'm a... sorry."

"For what? There's no need to be. We love you, Sam. Enjoy your night."

It was so kind of her to act dumb and say I had no reason to be sorry, but it made it worse. It made me feel that I was that much more of a horrible person and I was agonizing over the whole thing. Now, it would put me in a sour mood with Sarah. I went for a walk to try to cool down, collect my thoughts and keep myself from doing something stupid. That's when the second call came.

"Hey, Sarah!" The excitement dripped from my words.

"Sam, how are you?" Her words were eager and enticing.

We chatted briefly, catching up on the day before I ventured to double check the night's plans.

"So, are we still on for our movie tonight?"

"Well, see, Sam, that's the thing." Those words stopped me dead. What could it be this time? I couldn't handle anymore. "I forgot my other friends ..." -- there she went with her "other friends," whatever that meant -- "... invited me over to their place. I forgot it was tonight, you won't be mad if I go there for awhile first?" Nice assumption, I thought, trapping me.

She continued, "I just told them awhile ago I could. We can get together after, or spend all day Saturday together, it'll be even better that way!"

I was boiling. I could not believe her. Nothing made me furious like having plans that get changed at the last minute, especially something I was looking forward to so much. Damn it! But I couldn't be too mad at her, she seemed to have some kind of spell on me. But I didn't want to hurt her, and she seemed sincere.

"Yeah, that's totally fine, no big deal," I managed to get out the words, soaked in disappointment. She had to be completely oblivious not to pick up on it, but she ignored all the clues.

"Ok, great! Well, I can't wait to hang out. I'll call you later!" and she hung up.

This day was horrible, especially since I had treated Pops and Gran so badly. Now I could have spent time with them, and suddenly I wanted nothing more than for them to be here and for us to be together. That's what I get, I guessed. I imagined it was some test from God, and I failed big. I always fail big; I don't deserve to spend time with anyone, anyway. I just wanted to go row, escape and not come back. I momentarily thought about driving home and going out on the sea, but laziness got the better of me and I went back to the room. I felt so miserable, I wanted D to be gone; I didn't want to be around anyone, especially him. Slowly I opened the door, and my rage was back as he was just sitting there gaming on his computer.

"Sam! There you are!" he eagerly exclaimed.

"What's up, dude," I said clearly agitated.

"You got plans for tonight?"

I just let out a brief sigh.

"Well you should come out with me tonight, it'll be great. My buddy is having a bunch of people over to his house. There'll be pong, lots of beer. Shit! Everything!"

It would be the epitome of all the things I hated, social situations, things that make already annoying people even that much more so and I just wanted to shrink away and be alone, but surprisingly, at this moment, it was appealing. I had never drunk, but it seemed as though today was a perfect day to start. Of course, the real reason, the compelling reason behind why I told D I would love to go with him was that I hoped Sarah would be there. Maybe this was the party her "other friends" were going to. This could be my chance to accidently catch her. Maybe I could make her jealous of me and make her regret reneging on our plans for the night. So, actually, I was excited to go and I was going to go big.

We waited because that's what D told me we were supposed to do and well after the sun had set, D and I loaded up in my Jeep and drove to his friend's house. There were a lot of cars outside and momentarily I regretted my decision. I was nervous and had no idea what to expect. Trying to lag behind D, hopefully not being noticed, I walked very slowly to the door. D knocked, and a curious face peaked through the blinds of a window nearby. A bedraggled looking guy, who was exactly what I pictured when I thought of D's friends, opened the door, arms wide open with a plastic cup of beer in his hand. "D! My boy's finally here! And you brought a newbie. Good to have you..."

"Sam," D answered for me.

"Sam, my man, the name's Jay, welcome to my place," this was followed by D and Jay doing a handshake, followed by shouting, "D-Jay!"

Inside the place was bare, some old furniture, but nothing on the walls. It was pretty clean. There was a giant TV surrounded by several gaming systems in the living room. I scanned the room eagerly, hoping to see Sarah. I was disappointed; there were about six guys and not a single girl. They all had beer and one was behind the counter in the kitchen.

"This is Sam, he's D's roommate. Line up two more shot glasses, Kyle!"

They all looked up. I was nervous, but they seemed welcoming and friendly. The guy at the counter grabbed two more shot glasses from a shelf. All the shot glasses lined up were different; they seemed to be collected from a variety of places. He grabbed a bottle, with a golden liquid inside. Filling all the shot glasses, he called out, "It's on, boys!"

I was nervous, with no idea how to take a shot, having never done it before. It wasn't that I didn't want to, but I knew I would do something wrong and look dumb.

"What is it?" I blurted out, immediately regretting the choice.

The boys all laughed, but eventually realizing I wasn't joking. "It's whiskey, man," one of them shared.

"You ever done a shot?" Jay inquired.

I thought about lying, but for some reason I trusted these guys. At the moment, I wondered if Ben had ever had a shot. I never saw him drinking or heard him mention anything about it. I knew honesty would be best.

"I've never drunk before."

"Are you against it?" He asked sincerely.

"No, not at all. I want to, I just never have before."

"Ok, well, you're with the right boys for that!"

I was relieved to hear that.

"Don't worry, we'll take you under our wing. Take a shot as fast as you can, just gulp it down and feel like a man. ... Gentlemen raise your glasses!," Jay lifted his, proposing a toast. I nervously held mine up, "Here's to Sam! Welcome to the club, the start of many more!" Some of the guys responded, "To Sam," and everyone threw back the shot. I hesitated and watched them first. My insides cringed, the whiskey was the worst thing I had ever tasted. I quickly swallowed and did everything I could to hide the bitter face.

"Chase it with this," D said, handing me a beer. Compared to the taste of the whiskey, the beer was delicious, I gulped down several swallows to clear the remnant of the whiskey. At the moment for the first time in a long time, Sarah was far from my mind, and it was very liberating. Some guys started playing beer pong. I avoided that and I went out on the porch with D and Jay. As far away from my mind as Sarah was, suddenly Ben came charging into my memory. I wished he were here; I missed our times spent together in the summer. As the night passed on, I had several more beers and was in the middle of telling a story about a fishing trip Ben and I had gone on last summer when I got a phone call. It was Sarah. I jumped up and went out on the porch to answer it. I couldn't believe I had completely forgotten about her, and suddenly a wave of guilt washed over me; how could I so easily have done that.

I answered, "Hey, Sarah, how is your party?" I did my best to not show jealousy and to seem cool and collected. It must have worked because for the first time, I felt I had the upper hand.

"It's fun, where are you?"

"Oh, I just went out with my roommate and some guys." I had never gone out before, and I could tell she suddenly wanted to even the score.

"Well, want to come over? I'm heading back to my room."

My mind clouded over. I knew I couldn't drive, my mind clearly was not normal. I knew I was either buzzed or drunk, but having experienced neither before I didn't know. It wouldn't be that long a walk back, and I wanted to see her more than anything, I wanted to be with her. Suddenly all of the excitement and novelty of my new friends was gone and I wanted to escape to Sarah.

"Yeah, I'll have to walk back, but I should be there in like fifteen or twenty minutes?"

"You have to walk back?" she laughed, "Wow, Sam, sounds like you're living a little. Let me know when you're here." With that she hung up.

Walking back into Jay's, I announced, "Thanks so much for having me over, guys, but I gotta run."

After brief but annoying teasing about the suddenness of my departure, the guys thanked me for coming; all of them were a lot more drunk than I was. The caution I used was due to my lack of experience. Before I left, a clearly drunk Jay insisted I take an unopened bottle of whiskey as a, "welcome to the world of drinking," present as he termed it. My refusal was futile, and I walked out the door into the Maine night with the first alcohol I had ever owned. Knowing I couldn't walk back to school with whiskey, I decided to stow it in my Jeep. I wrapped it in a blanket I had under my seat and walked towards Sarah.

The cool night air felt great. I hadn't realized I had been sweating at Jay's. I hoped Sarah wouldn't care that I had been drinking. Who knows, maybe she wouldn't even notice. The thought of Sarah caused me to quicken my pace. It was short of a jog but quicker than a walk. Amazingly, my prediction had been right and I reached Sarah's dorm within twenty minutes. She came down and let me in. The night was quiet and hardly anyone was around. She came to the door in a Bowdoin hoodie and a little pair of shorts. Smiling at how cute she looked, I wrapped my arms around her and gave her a big hug.

"What a friendly hello," she teased, "Are you drunk?"

"No, I'm just feeling good, and excited to see you."

She took my hand and led me to her room. I had been there once or twice before, briefly, picking her up. That time had been spent sitting on her couch, waiting. Well, as soon as she closed the door behind me she turned, put her hands on my head and pressed her lips to mine. I was taken off guard. We had never kissed before. For a while, I would longingly look at her lips but I never allowed it to progress beyond that point. I allowed myself to believe the reasoning behind this was that I wanted to get to know Sarah better, and not let the physical aspect of our relationship get in the way of the deeper things. But now here we were, my first real kiss, and I liked it. My arms wrapped around her and I pulled her in close. Why had I put this off for so long? As we kissed we slowly walked towards the couch. I seemed to be on autopilot, instincts I had never tested before took over.

Sarah pulled away momentarily and I was afraid I had done something wrong. But, no, she took off her hoodie and revealed her bareness underneath. I looked in awe as I beheld a naked woman for the first time in my life. Without realizing it, I took my shirt off, too, and we returned to kissing, with hands exploring the beauty of each other. It was all so new, so exciting to me, I wasn't even thinking about what I was doing -- I was just doing. She began to unbutton my pants as I pulled her shorts off. For the first time I was completely vulnerable with another human being. It felt so right. I never felt so trusted and I never trusted so. She lay back on the couch and I gave myself to her fully in that moment of passion. Her eyes opened and she looked at me, it felt as though she looked deep into my soul and she uttered, "I love you." I was completely hers and she was completely mine.

When the moment was over, she laid her head on my chest, our arms wrapped around each other and we stayed silent in that embrace for awhile. Moments after the act had passed, my sense of logic and reason suddenly rushed into my head. Holy shit! That just happened! The peace of the moment was swept far, far away by the fear of the future and chaos took control. I felt guilty, as though I had caused her to do something she didn't want to do. In the midst of many other fears I thought, "What if she gets pregnant?" Surprised that it had taken so long to cross my mind, I was tempted to ask Sarah, but seeing her so seemingly at peace, I figured I would save it for another time. A storm of worries and regrets were warring inside me and here Sarah was so at peace. It was true I had never felt so loved or one with another person, but I was tormented by it regardless. A mental image of my getting up and rowing away, into the sea and leaving these worries behind gave me relief from the thoughts. I pictured the waves crashing on the boat and spraying me with their cool mist, the gentle rock of the boat and the seabirds flying over head. The thought of the shore slowly disappeared and peace fell on me. Sarah's lips on my chest, startled me awake and brought me quickly back to reality. She began to kiss me again and everything was ok, I was at peace in the real world now. The countless worries, thoughts, and fears of the previous moment were gone and the raw, unrestrained, freedom of each other had taken its place.

I awoke the next day with Sarah in her bed, unable to believe how many firsts had occurred the previous night. She was still asleep, so I lay there quietly reflecting. The night seemed to happen very fast and my memories were more of a blur than distinct moments. I think if I had tried I could have convinced myself it hadn't happened. I felt as though I should do something for Sarah, I wanted the morning to be special; I wanted to be good to her. I thought of getting donuts and coffee, but there were many flaws in that plan, the main one being that I would be locked out of her building if I left. Also, I did not even want to risk the appearance of her waking up and my being gone. I suddenly remembered my truck was at Jay's, too. That was annoying because I would have to pick it up. For a second, I was afraid that maybe my car had been searched by the police and that they discovered the whiskey and I would be in serious trouble. But the ridiculousness of those thoughts took care of them. I decided to just wake her and go together. I moved the hair from her face and tucked it behind her ear and gently kissed her on the cheek, making a noise just loud enough to rouse her.

She turned to me and I had never seen her so beautiful. Her tired green eyes, looking up at me so contented. Her hair was everywhere and sticking up, and her makeup was worn. But her smile was sweet.

"Good morning," she cheerfully uttered before closing her eyes.

As she rested a little bit more, I imagined what Ben's reaction would be if I were to share the events of the previous night. Would he be proud, or disappointed? I wasn't sure. All I could picture was his stroking that great beard of his as he listened quietly as he did so well. I knew whether or not he agreed with the course the night had taken, he wouldn't make me feel guilty or bad about it. He never made me feel bad or guilty about anything. I hoped that one day other people would feel the same about me.

Sarah sat up and yawned, "Good morning."

"Good second morning," I laughed.

I proposed a trip to Dunkin'' and she heartily agreed. We both readied ourselves to go out in public and did our best to wake up. It wasn't long before we made our way to Dunkin'. Neither of us mentioned the night before. We were just two people together in the moment. That's one thing I liked about Sarah, she was alive in the moment, she didn't dwell in the past or get too caught up on the future. She was living in the here and now, and I felt as though I was more alive when I was with her. After coffee, we walked hand in hand and picked up my car from Jay's. All the other cars were still there from the night before.

I didn't realize it then but that was the start of a whole new era in my relationship with Sarah. There wasn't a specific talk or discussion about it, but from then on it was understood she was my girlfriend and I her boyfriend. I never had wanted someone before in my life and now I had someone and I could not be happier about it. I found myself mentioning her every time I talked with Pops and Gran or Ben. I never gave them the details of our relationship. I figured that wasn't important, but they knew she was important to me by the amount of time I devoted to her in my calls. Ben would always caution me, so I found myself speaking less of her to him and naturally speaking less to him at all.

From that day on, our relationship was increasingly physical. It seemed we were always having sex. It was funny to me that it had gone from something I had never done to something that was an active part of my life. It seemed so fitting, because we were so close and it was the only way to express how deeply we felt about each other. It was the only way to be vulnerable and the only way to show the true extent of our feelings. We also regularly confessed our love to each other. We were together very often but we still had her "other friends." It wasn't as bad now when she would go out with her "other friends" as I would go out with D, Jay and the boys. We would drink and they prided themselves on the amount they were able to build my tolerance. Sarah never hung out with my friends and I never hung out with her friends. We were either together alone or with other people. We really had no mutual friends. Life seemed good.

But as much as that was an escape, I was still tormented. Anytime she would deny me sex, I would be so hurt and wonder what I had done. I never pushed her but sometimes we would start kissing and then she would just stop. That bothered me because I always assumed I had done something wrong and never knew what it could have been. It had a power over me. Whenever she would do things with her friends and I wouldn't, those nights were the worst. I wanted nothing more than to call her every five minutes and check up on her. As much as I hated to admit it, I hoped she would always have a bad night whenever she did things with other people. Those nights were agonizing and I always imagined she would fall away from me, that I would royally screw it up and completely ruin the relationship. Through the course of our relationship, she would mention other guys, the guys who were in her other group of friends. I knew nothing about them, but I hated them and did not trust them. A couple of times I brought it up to Sarah and she would not have it. She accused me of being jealous and insecure and it would always lead to a huge fight. I never had peace when we were fighting, but it seemed to happen more and more often. When we did fight, I would persist in making sure everything was resolved before we fell asleep. That caused some late nights. Often times she would never give up any ground and I would cede to her in order to bring about such peace. It bothered me, but I was just happy for things to be good again.

One time I asked her if she was worried she would get pregnant. She told me she was on birth control, and that planted a seed of distrust that grew within me. I assumed that meant from the first night she was on birth control, and why would she have needed to be? I wanted to ask her, but I never did. I never ever brought it up again, but I did allow it to slowly eat at me and poison me when I was alone. It used to be that I loved being alone, but now when I was alone, that was when I was afraid and disturbed. People, mostly Sarah, became a distraction, and when I couldn't be around her I would be around the boys and drink.

It seemed that the bad was easier to focus on, but still, for the most part, things were really good. We were closer than ever, and on most occasions were incredibly happy. We loved our times together and the relationship seemed to be progressing. The bad moments happened, maybe once or twice in an average week, but the other times were smooth sailing, because I loved Sarah and she loved me.

SEVEN

The year continued on. When a routine is set, time has a tendency to pass by without our really noticing, and I had developed just such a rut with my life in my freshman year. It seemed as though time was passing like a train down the tracks. I just didn't see where I was going.

I had a couple of weekends that I spent at home and I also went home for the holidays. During these times at home, I was never really completely there. My mind was always with Sarah and most of the hours were spent on the phone with her. I could never let myself just be. At the start of the year, I had looked forward to going home and going out in *Santiago*, but when the chance came, I always decided I would rather just lie in bed and talk to Sarah. Ben invited me to go fishing a couple of times and I always passed up those chances, too. The slowest times were the ones away from Sarah. I couldn't picture life without her. The longest we ever went without seeing each other that first year was probably four days, at most. Also, after that first time, our relationship became more and more physical and sex became a regular routine for us. My life had become something I would never ever have imagined or even dreamed and I was happy. I felt safe. It was secure enough and I hardly ever thought about the past, all the memories and scars that had tormented me for years were now distant objects compared to the love that consumed me.

Then, as life also has a tendency to do, just when I was really beginning to get comfortable, the future began to rear its head around the corner. That future was summer, something that for so long had been a salvation. Now it represented the horror of being away from Sarah. It became an ever growing worry of mine. I just wanted freshman year to never end. It seemed that the more I tried to slow it down, the faster time would go by. I never brought the subject up with Sarah, I guess I was figuring that not thinking about something could make it not real. Well, unfortunately, I discovered that life doesn't work that way. It was eventually brought to the surface, but not by me. Sarah brought it up one night about a month before school let out.

It was one of those rare days when the sun is out and the day is suddenly warmer. A day like that seemed even rarer that spring. So obviously we could not pass up all the opportunities that went with it, and we decided to take a walk to the coast. Hand in hand, we walked quietly along a favorite route of ours. As we were both taking in the scenery on such a beautiful day, not many words were spoken on the walk out to the beach. Sarah did at one point look up to me and say,

"You're too good to me Sam. Why are you so amazing?"

Of course, I thought of myself as anything but amazing, but her comment made me feel so loved and needed. It made me feel that I was doing something right and it wasn't often that I felt like that. Never the kind to just accept a compliment without trying to return the favor, I conjured up the awkward response,

"Well, you're inspiring."

She just smiled and looked up towards the sky as we continued on our way. The walk had become a favorite of ours, and we passed all the familiar places. The birds seemed overjoyed with the warmth and were out in large numbers. I watched them as they flew overhead and wondered how the birds in each flock knew one another. Were they family, or was it friends perhaps, maybe just completely random groups? How long do they stay together? How long did they live? My mind ran off with the birds but Sarah brought me back.

"Sit with me, Sam." she sat down on a large rock with the waves breaking not far below. I did as she requested and put my hand on her back. She turned to me and smiled.

"Will we be together forever?"

I don't know why but the question made me so happy. I guess I figured no one would want to be with me that long and I had the underlying fear of losing Sarah.

"Yeah, forever."

My words seemed inadequate to express what I felt in my heart, but the kiss from Sarah on my cheek settled any fear I had of her not understanding the extent of my feeling. I so longed to bring up summer and being apart, but it felt so negative and I never was good with negative. I opened my mouth, "Sarah…" but the words didn't come.

"What is it, Sam?"

"Nothing, never mind," I tried to move on as I looked out at the boats, suddenly wishing I was out on *Santiago*.

"You were going to say something, Sam!"

"It's just, … I'm going to miss you this summer." I said it, got it off my chest. Once the words came they didn't stop, "It'll be so hard to not see you everyday."

"But you'll be with me, even if we're not together. Sam, I'll think about you all the time. Think about how in love we'll be when next year comes and we're together again. We're not that far away, either. We'll still see each other a lot."

I understood what she was trying to do, but it bugged me that she didn't seem bothered by it. It almost seemed okay, or like something she was looking forward to. Was I making it out to be something bigger than it was? I didn't know, but she must have sensed my anxiety.

"Sam, I am going to love you forever, and we will be together no matter what. This summer will be hard, but it's going to make us so much stronger. Our love will grow so much. My love for you will never wane, it's only going to get stronger, and I can't wait to see how strong it is when we finally have everyday together again," and placing her hand on the side of my head, she leaned in and kissed me. For a moment, I was looking forward to the distance. She was right, our love could grow and strengthen. The rest of the afternoon, we walked the shore and looked at the tied-up boats. We took a nap together and I was genuinely happy.

That night I called Ben and asked him if he thought love could last forever. He said, "Without a doubt," and I sensed the conviction in his voice. I wondered why he didn't have a girlfriend. I mean, other than that massive beard of his, it seemed as though he was very knowledgeable about women. I was sure he could make someone very happy, and I felt bad for him always being alone. I wished he could have someone to make him happy.

The school year flew by and before I knew it, I was helping Sarah move out on our last day together. As was typical, I tried to fill my mind with distractions to avoid the truth of the finality the moment presented. Sarah had already packed most of her things; it was my job to carry the loads out to her car and get it all to fit. I took on the challenge eagerly because I had always felt it was proof of manliness if you could pack things in a car well. It was frustrating work and several times I had to hide my failures, but after relentless effort I finally got it all packed in with enough room for Sarah to drive. Expecting a long drawn out goodbye and maybe even a walk along the coast, I was taken aback when she told me she better go ahead and hit the road. It seemed she was eager to leave and I was hurt and scared. I don't know if it was purposeful or not, but I immediately shut down and got quiet. She seemed not to notice though. She wrapped her arms around me and kissed me. I could not help but kiss back, as much as I wanted to throw her arms down and away from me and be mad at her. The desire to hold her and never let go was just as strong.

"I love you, Sam. You're the most amazing guy ever and I swear I don't deserve you at all," she whispered into my ear. "I am going to miss you, but we'll be so strong after this summer." She kissed me once more and pulled herself away, getting in her car. With a honk and a wave, she drove off out of sight. I was devastated. For days, even weeks, I had been picturing our final goodbye and in every instance in my dream it was a lot longer and a lot more satisfying. It seemed like such a cheap way to end an amazing semester and I was scared of what was next. I wanted to wallow in the sorrow, but decided I might as well get home to a distraction as quick as possible. I had packed up my Jeep the night before so I walked to my car, got in, and drove back towards Camden. I hadn't been on the road long when I broke down. I don't know where it came from, but it seemed the tears just began to pour. I attempted to fight them back, but was overwhelmed. I let go and released it in a wave of emotion, heaving and sobbing like a child, I didn't even care if the other drivers saw me. After several minutes of flooding tears, I wiped my eyes, tightened my grip on the wheel, and drove home.

When I arrived, Pops and Gran had planned a surprise dinner and had invited Ben to join us. As I pulled into the driveway, I saw all three of them come spilling from the front door. Ben stood back as Gran walked toward me with arms outstretched and I eagerly fell into them. She kissed me on my cheek and whispered gently, "Welcome home, Love."

Pops put an arm around Gran and one around me and in that embrace I fell apart again. Without warning the emotions swarmed back into me and I wept there in their arms. At first I was embarrassed, mainly because I didn't want Ben to think I was a softy. But I couldn't help it. I don't know how long I spent there, but Gran gently swayed and kept whispering over and over again, "Welcome home, Love." I felt very much at home at that moment. Finally, I was able to collect myself and I looked up to Ben, hoping my eyes weren't nearly as red and swollen as I knew they were. He just smiled at me which was exaggerated by his bushy beard. His eyes seemed more watery than normal and I felt for a moment he was jealous of me. Perhaps he was jealous of the embrace I just shared. There seemed to be pain in him, and I was very perplexed. But soon Pops ushered us all inside and we sat down and enjoyed a great cheerful meal and evening coffee together afterwards. That night I fell asleep better than I had in months.

The immediate peace of returning home was not to last, though. Barely hours into the next morning, I was missing Sarah and wishing I was still at school, knowing she was near, knowing what she was doing and knowing that she loved me. I worried that she didn't even miss me and that she had already forgotten about me. I spent the entire day fighting the urge to call her. I realized it might be a mistake to request a couple days off before I starting going back to work with Ben. Work would have been a distraction and definitely would have kept me from being able to call her. But, no, laziness got the best of me, thus opening the door for torment. Agony and torment, all day long, never ceasing -- was this how separation from love was supposed to feel? I had an uneasiness that consumed every moment. My heart always seemed to be fluttering with fear, I was always on the verge of being light headed, and I was consumed with checking for missed calls from Sarah. The day was awful. I was never fully anywhere. Conversation with Pops or Gran was impossible with my mind far off, worrying what Sarah was doing. If I went for a walk, all I could think about were the walks I had gone on with Sarah. At one point, when I was out on a walk trying to clear my mind, I fell into a bed of pine needles. I put my hands to my head and let out a deep and sorrowful sigh. I wondered how long and dreadful the summer I had in store would be. I couldn't handle this; I needed to talk to Ben and get some advice.

I called him and it went straight to his voicemail. I had forgotten that just because I wasn't working didn't mean he wasn't working. This offered no comfort and now with every ring of the phone, I got excited that it would be either Sarah or Ben, yet all day long it was neither. Around dinner time, the loud ring of the phone burst the silence of dinner. I just about jumped out of my seat with the noise.

"Settle, Boy," said Pops with humor that was totally lost on me.

It had to be Sarah, finally. It seemed like forever since we had talked and every waking minute of the day for me had been consumed with waiting for this moment when I could finally have peace. I anticipated hearing about her day, hearing how much she missed me and how she wished the school year had never ended. My fantasy was cut short by Gran.

"Sam, it's for you!"

I smiled as I left the room. The phone was down on the counter and I picked it up, "Hey, Baby!"

"Uh… well that's a first but, I'm doing pretty well. And you, Princess?"

Oh gosh, it was Ben. Not only was this a huge disappointment, but it also was incredibly embarrassing to not only call Ben "Baby," but for him to know I called Sarah that. I was silent on my end, I just wanted to hang up and scream. Now I regretted calling Ben in the first place. As my thoughts started down the road of no return, Ben broke the silence,

"You're doing OK today, man?"

"Well, uh … it's just that … I dunno, never mind." I wanted to scream it at him, I wanted to spill my heart over the phone and complain and vent, but I couldn't get it out.

"Well, if you're down, I was thinking about getting some coffee in town. I could pick you up on my way, catch up a little bit?"

That was exactly the thing I needed. I eagerly agreed and he confirmed plans, "Well, I'll be there in five to ten minutes, Babe," followed by a big laugh, "I'm sorry, man. I couldn't resist that one. See you soon!"

Why the hell did he have to end the conversation that way? I hung up the phone and threw it as hard as I could at the couch, immediately regretting the decision but glad my aim was on and it landed unharmed on the cushions. It was so frustrating to me that I could only focus on the negative, the joke he was making about "Babe." I didn't at all focus on the fact that he knew something was on my mind and had so generously offered to go out. I knew when he called, he wasn't planning on getting coffee, at least I didn't think he was.

He arrived and we were on our way. Ben broke the ice, "So, rough day, man?"

"You pretty much guessed it," I responded.

"Miss the girl?"

"How'd you know?" I asked suspiciously.

"I know what it's like to be up all night because you miss a girl so bad, to think about her all day and miss her."

The way he talked about it had a much different feel than what I had experienced that day.   There was a certain feeling of happiness and peace unlike the agony I could relate to. Ben's tear-choked voice broke my thoughts, "I know what it's like to miss a girl every single day." His eyes were welling up with tears. He quickly looked out the driver's side window. I had never seen him so emotional. I realized we weren't talking about the same thing, but I knew it didn't matter, talking to Ben would make it better and that was the most important to me right now.

"What do I do to get by? I can't live every day this summer like I lived today."

"Well, first of all, I'm just happy you have someone to miss like that," he responded.

Once again I was pretty sure he didn't completely understand how I felt. It wasn't so much missing as agonizing and dreading that I wouldn't wish on anyone. I'm sure if he truly knew the extent of my pain he would have phrased his words differently. Before I could analyze everything too much we arrived at the coffee shop.

The barista was a girl about my age and she was absolutely beautiful. We walked in and she smiled at us as though we were long-lost friends. She had really dark hair, almost black and I could tell she was the "artsy" type. I liked her immediately, which didn't sit well with me. How could I like this complete stranger, who would have remained completely anonymous to me had I never set foot in this coffee shop? It wasn't fair to Sarah for me to like this girl, so I thought in my mind. Ben walked up to the counter and ordered first.

"Supreme coffee, room for cream and whatever my friend here wants," he motioned in my direction.

"And what would you like, friend?" She looked at me and I knew in another world and another time, I would have fallen for her. But not in the world I lived in. I loved Sarah and couldn't even let my thoughts go down that path.

"I'll be simple, I'll just take the exact same thing," I replied.

"Simple or boring?" She said with a laugh.

"Simply boring," Ben chimed in. It was as if he had a sense I was at a loss for words and I was glad for his interjection. We waited for our drinks and after doctoring them up, found a nice secluded spot on two easy chairs in a far corner. I was feeling bold. I'm not sure if it was the surge of energy from the coffee or the wave of love I felt for Sarah, after the barista had my mind spinning.

"Ben, today was horrible, it was agony, and I don't think it's the same agony you were talking about. I felt sick, almost nauseous." As I talked and the words continued to flow, I suddenly began to be taken over with shyness and felt my feelings slowly crawling back into wherever they so often hid within me.

"I'm sorry, Sam. Sounds like a rough day," he began. For some reason it angered me to hear him say that "…sounds like a rough day" It was horrible; "rough" didn't do it justice.

"Never an easy situation to be in," he continued on. "Have you figured out why it was like that? What made you feel that way?"

I sat there, my elbows on my legs and the coffee warming my hands, looking out into the darkness the window presented. It took me a while to formulate my thoughts and find the right words. Ben waited patiently; he seemed to have no feeling on his tongue because he was gulping his coffee before I could even sip mine without fear of getting burned. I was briefly distracted, wondering if one is born that way or if it's acquired through years of burning your tongue, because if so, I was well on my way.

"Well, I guess the best way to put it is," I tried to spit out my thoughts, "umm... the thought that kept tormenting me, well, I guess it was more of a fear." My words didn't seem to make any sense even to me; there was no way Ben would be able to make a lick of sense out of them. Regardless, I carried on; I knew I needed to get this off my chest.

"I'm afraid she'll forget about me. I'm afraid she'll find someone else and I'll sit here in love with her all summer while she loves someone else. I'm afraid she won't even know who I am next fall and I'll be alone again."

As I ran through my list of fears to Ben, my heart was racing. I felt angry and afraid. It was one of those moments when you don't realize how afraid you really are until you begin to open the gates to let your feelings flood out. Ben sat there listening until I had finished venting. He was a patient man, a quality I had always admired in him. He never seemed to rush into anything and had a sense of calm about him. Once again, I found myself wishing I was Ben. Life would be so much better and easier. People would like me more and I wouldn't be so afraid. It didn't seem fair to me at that moment that we didn't get to choose who we were before we entered this world. I watched Ben as he collected his thoughts in preparation for a response. I was glad it was he who had to offer advice and opinion to me, because I knew I wouldn't be able to help myself. The despair had built up to such a level that any answer would be disappointing. But if anyone had a chance, it was Ben.

"Are there any reasons you feel this way? Or are the thoughts just based on fear?"

I got mad that he had asked. I was mad and I'm sure it was obvious to Ben when I didn't answer his question and avoided eye contact, but a savior came in the form of the beautiful barista. We both saw her walking our way so we quickly did our best to appear cheerful.

"How are your coffees?"

I found it odd that she had come to just asked about coffee, but I didn't mind. She had a demeanor that made me relax and the anger and fear melted away.

"Delicious. I love a good strong brew," responded Ben with his signature bearded smile.

"How about yours, friend?" There she went with the "friend" again, and I loved it that she did.

"It's very good, thank you," I was not nearly as good with words as Ben. "Well, free refills on me tonight," she said with a wink in my direction.

"Thank you very much," Ben and I said almost in unison.

She walked away and Ben whispered over to me, "She likes you."

"There's no way she likes me!"

"I'm serious, Sam, I can just tell, why else do you think we got free refills?"

I looked up to the counter and she smiled before quickly turning to look the other way. Maybe he was right, maybe she did. I still found it hard to believe, but Ben knew his stuff. Even so, I was Sarah's boy and didn't need distractions or temptations like this.

" "Maybe it's just God reminding you that there are more girls out there, Sam, so as not to get so worked up over just one," he offered.

"Shut up, Ben! Don't ever say that again," I snapped before I turned and starred out the window. We sat there in silence for a while, neither willing to break the silence. After what felt like hours, even though it was just a matter of minutes, Ben finally broke it.

"I'm sorry, Sam. I should not have said that. I was only trying to make light of the situation."

"Well, Sarah is my girl and I wouldn't have anyone else, even if every girl in the world liked me. She's the only girl I want and I would take a thousand days of agony like today before I would have a day of bliss with someone else."

"Well, if that's the case, Sam, then show her that. Surprise her, be spontaneous. Think of some ways to prompt her to think about you this summer and focus that energy that has become fear on romantic thoughts and ideas. That is my only advice, and I wish you luck with that."

I appreciated his advice, but was still too mad from his previous statement to be able to show my appreciation or even respond. We sat there in silence, which was momentarily broken when Ben went up and got our coffees refilled. He seemed to be up there awhile and when he came back he offered a new topic.

"Looks like it'll be a good summer to go out in *Santiago*."

He knew how to get to me. As much as I didn't want to answer, the thought brought me cheer and the idea of escape seemed wonderful.

"Absolutely," I smiled.

That gave way to a pleasant conversation about summer possibilities as we finished our second cups of coffee. As we left, the barista offered an excited wave and bubbly goodbye. I was flattered and when Ben dropped me off, I was in a good mood. I was able to thank him for the advice and move on beyond what had angered me. I noticed that since I had moved to Maine, I seemed to be dealing with my anger more quickly. But that night I regretted the coffee. It seemed to keep me up for hours fighting a losing battle against my thoughts. I kept thinking of the barista, which was bad enough because it made me feel so guilty, but then I would picture who Sarah was meeting and falling for. The image of her flirting with someone else was agonizing. I lay in bed not sure whether or not I had fallen asleep until the sun began its morning journey.

I got up and went downstairs. Pops and Gran were both up, which kind of aggravated me, because I just wanted to escape, not get involved in any human contact. I quickly told them I was going rowing and left before they even had time to respond. I pictured their conversation in my head after I left, how they worried about me, and how I never seemed happy. I felt as though people were always talking about me behind my back. Whether it actually occurred or not, I'll never know. I went out to the boat house and got *Santiago*. It felt like I was freeing a bird from a cage. I was so excited to get back on the sea.

It was a little choppy this particular morning. Rowing in the wind and rough water would require extra effort which only made the ocean that much more enticing. I collected the oars, put the boat in the water and finally pushed away. My muscles quickly got sore. I had definitely gotten rusty and I was no longer used to the rhythm of the strokes, but I was glad to be free and fought through it. Joy came to me as I rowed out and the shore shrank away. This truly felt like home. The lack of sleep the previous night was definitely getting to me. I was very sleepy, but I knew even if I tried there was no way I'd be able to sleep.

As I rowed on the tossing sea an idea came to me. I should take Ben's advice and surprise Sarah that very day. I would buy her flowers and drive down to her house and sweep her off her feet. The idea was so exciting and as I rowed throughout the bay, I formulated the plan over and over again in my head. I would be such a hero. I pictured her running into my arms and kissing me. Who knows? Maybe she'd even invite me to spend the night. In my favorite version, she would admit how agonizing the days had been for her and how much she missed me and thought of me constantly. I could brag about how much she meant to me and how true I was to her. I stretched out in *Santiago,* letting the waves gently toss me around while the soreness in my arms diminished enough to row back to shore.

After I pulled the boat from the water I went into the house and declared my plan to Gran. Pops had gone into town for some errands. She assured me it was a cute idea. Not exactly the words I wanted to hear, but I was happy to have any reassurance I could get. Gran actually gave me five dollars and told me to buy nicer flowers than I had planned. I showered up and had a brief lunch with Gran before I was on the road in my Jeep, driving down to see Sarah. At the florist, a kind lady helped me pick a large lively bouquet full of scents and colors that she promised were sure to please any girl. I placed them on the passenger seat and found myself looking over at them every several minutes, so pleased and excited. In a matter of time, I would be back with Sarah and life would be at peace again.

The drive to Sarah's house went by quickly and it didn't take much effort for me to find it. It was secluded, not far off the road and surrounded by trees. A car was parked in the driveway. I knew it wasn't hers. It must have been her parents'. I thought they both worked all day, but I was too excited to think much of it. I didn't want to block the drive so I parked on the street. Looking in the rearview mirror, I checked my teeth and fixed my hair. Taking a deep breath, I grabbed the flowers and spruced up their shape and got out. I walked towards the door, not really taking anything in. I was shaking from my nerves, but excited to see Sarah. As I was almost to the house, parallel with the car, I glanced over and suddenly realized it was occupied. There, in the backseat was Sarah and my greatest fear hit me all at once. She was there and happily kissing some other guy. So into it with her eyes closed that she didn't even see me standing there.

I lost all feeling and didn't even notice the flowers fall to my feet. Tears rushed to my eyes and before I knew what was happening, I had fallen to my knees and was slowly falling forward onto the ground. My mind was utterly blank. Then an excruciating mental pain overwhelmed me. Everything was spinning and the world seemed to be in slow motion. This hurt suddenly outweighed all others I had felt in my life while simultaneously bringing them all to the forefront of my mind. I needed to escape. I needed to get out of there. The image of her kissing that man would forever be seared into my mind. I could not shake it and she seemed so happy and at peace. I tried to get to my feet and was doing all I could to avoid looking at the car, but the strength it took was more than I had.

I looked and saw Sarah's panicked face and our eyes met, boring a wound deeper into me. She opened the door as she was buttoning her shirt which only added to the agony, "Oh my god, Sam, why are you here!" I had no words, no thoughts, only pain and horrible images in my mind, but her getting out of that car gave me the strength I needed. I shook my head and I took off in a sprint towards my Jeep, hopping in and driving off without a look back at the flowers lying there in the yard. All I could see was Sarah, joyfully kissing that guy and finally the tears were accompanied with sobs. I drove home so fast, I don't even remember a single detail of the trip. All I know was that somewhere in the mess of images and pain, a different image popped into my mind: the bottle of whiskey was somewhere in my Jeep. I hadn't thought about it since that party, but it was under one of my seats. All I could think about was drinking that entire bottle and forgetting everything. That was it. I would run off as soon as I got back. I would drink the bottle and then take *Santiago* out and never return. Never before had such an idea sounded so sweet. As soon as I was in the driveway, I fell out of the car and began to scrounge around under the seats looking for the whiskey. I found it and as I shut the door, I heard Gran's voice.

"How did it go, Sam dear?" She was sincere and standing on the porch.

I couldn't even look at her though.

"Don't talk to me!" I screamed as I ran off into the forest with my whiskey. I ran for about 100 yards before I finally fell back against a tree and took my first swig. Unscrewing the cap, I poured the the whiskey into my mouth and it spilled out onto my cheeks. Not even caring to wipe my face clean, I took another swig. It was bitter and it burned, but I was thankful for that pain. A pleasant distraction from the mental pain I was in the grip of at the moment. I wept like a child as my mind raced between Sarah kissing whoever that guy was, and standing there asking why I was there. I was so hurt. I found it odd that I wasn't furious, in a rage, that I didn't try to hurt the guy or even think of that. Anger was nowhere, I finally found something that would drown my anger. Great and utter mental pain. Another taste of whiskey as soon as I could fit it between sobs. Had I the capacity for logical thought, I'm sure I would have wondered why Gran didn't attempt to find me, with her tendency to worry about me and the obvious state of distress I was in when I returned.

For a while I sat there, sobbing, not wanting to close my eyes and increase the screen for the images that were so tormenting, yet it was so hard to keep them open. More sips of whiskey. I needed to finish the bottle so I could escape out to sea and, hopefully, it would consume me and I would never have to deal with this dreadful life again. I didn't know it was possible to cry so much. I had nothing to look forward to. I had no one in my life. Why had Sarah followed the path of all the others I had opened myself up to? Why did I open myself up to her and take that chance? I wondered how many guys she had done stuff with while we were together. Was this the first or had there been other men all along. I was nothing.

Still unaware of my surroundings I was more than startled to hear Ben's voice. "Sam, what happened? Are you OK?"

I looked up at him through tearful eyes and just took another deep swig of whiskey. This time I held the bottle to my lips and gulped three times. Glancing up, I realized Ben' eyes were full of tears, too. He reached down and easily wrestled the bottle out of my hands and quickly poured the remaining whiskey on the ground.

I yelled, "No!" as I dove to try to catch the spill in my mouth.

"Don't ever try to solve your problems with alcohol, Sam, trust me. I ruined my life for five years with that poisonous remedy."

He sat down next to me against the great pine and wrapped his arms around me. "Whatever happened, Sam, I'm so sorry."

That was all he said as his arms held me close. I turned my head into his arm and wept uncontrollably. He held me without words and without moving until I finally had cried my ducts dry. I pulled away and sat there rubbing my eyes.

"It hurts so bad, Ben," I managed to say.

"I know pain, Sam, I really do, and I'm so sorry."

I couldn't help but laugh when he said he knew pain. He knew nothing of my life, nothing of my childhood, he had no idea how hurt I was. How dare he? The small seed grew into anger and I pulled away and I don't know if it was the pain or whiskey that emboldened me, but my guess it was both, but the anger dripped forth from my lips.

"You know pain? You think you know pain, Ben? Do you know what it's like to never know your dad? Huh? Do you know how it feels to live your entire life without a dad and the only thing you know is you were the reason he disappeared and left everyone. All the pain it caused Pops and Gran when he disappeared and left my mom was because of me. Me being born!" I laughed a hurtful laugh, "No one has seen or heard from him since, and that was just the start. You know what it's like to get molested by your step dad and feel so dirty and wrong and angry. To watch your mom as she supports him and be so hurt as she loves him and he hurts you. Do you know what that feels like, Ben? To finally get taken out of that situation, to fall in love and go to surprise the one you love so much to find her in a car making out with someone else, do you know how that feels? Do you know what it's like to have those images forever in your mind? Do you think you know pain, Ben?"

By the time my rant was over, I was shouting and heaving and the tears were back and I fell face first on the ground pounding my fists.

Ben approached without saying anything and attempted to put his hand on my back. I angrily jerked away.

"You're right, Sam. I don't know that kind of pain. I don't at all. I had no idea on your past and it breaks my heart to hear that, but I do know loss and the pain it causes. My senior year of college, right before graduation, my fiancée and parents were driving up together to surprise me and they got in a car accident and all three died that night. I lost everyone I had and cared about and loved that night, Sam. I turned to alcohol and drank everyday for five years. My life was nothing. I lost every job I got and would just drink. My health was horrible and I was so hurt. Finally, one day I was looking at pictures at the start of another binge and realized I was dishonoring all those I loved who were killed. I pulled myself together and moved here to Maine. There isn't a day that goes by that I don't miss each and every one of them. I know what it's like to feel guilty, too. I felt like it was my fault because they were all driving to visit me. So, yes, I know pain."

Looking up at Ben's eyes, filled with tears, I could see the agony and I could see the pain, but he was a fool: He had love and belonging and yes, they were dead, but he had them at one point.

"And your fiancée, she cheated on you? And your parents hated you and hurt you and made you unhuman?"

"No, Sam, you're right. They were wonderful. My parents were the best and most loving people I have ever known and my fiancée was a saint and cared about me deeply. But I still lost them."

"But you had them, Ben. And now you're hiding away in Maine behind that stupid beard of yours." I had always admired his beard, but now I hated it. "Is that what you're doing, hiding behind that beard? 'Cause you think you know pain? You're a fool, Ben. At least you were loved, at least you were loved!"

"Is that better? To have lost them forever? You think so? Huh, Sam? Well, you have wonderful grandparents and that barista the other night liked you and gave me her number to give you, but you're so consumed with yourself, you give no thought to anyone around you. Gran called me 'cause she was worried about you, and so I came to find you. I didn't have to come out here, but Sam, I care about you. I like you. You hurt me really deep tonight, but I know it's because you're hurting and that's ok, I forgive you. Just know that you are loved and cared about even if you don't see it."

I looked up at him and without remorse uttered the words I would forever regret, "I hate you, Ben."

I had hurt a lot of people in my lifetime and I had never seen it so evidenced as I did on Ben's face at that moment. He was stunned. His mouth fell open and he stared at me expressionlessly. He slowly backed away and, overwhelmed with hurt, he fell back against another tree. I couldn't handle it. Rising to my feet, I ran toward the house, stumbling the whole way, rushing to my room, ignoring Pops and Gran, and slamming the door behind me, I fell into my bed and with the help of the whiskey, sleep finally took hold of me.

EIGHT

Now, here I was some thirteen years later, back in Maine again, looking back on a turbulent past and a time I hadn't allowed myself to think about in years. Two of the principle figures in my life were now dead, most recently Ben and also Pops, who had preceded him only seven years before. It's weird how much life can change in a matter of just a few years. Friendships are made and lost, the people who are part of your everyday life are seen only a couple times a year, and death never hesitates to steal those we love the most.

Hemingway bounded onto my lap and kept poking his big wet nose into my chest longing for a good behind -the-ear rub. This brought me completely back to the present moment. After the long look back, I realized I needed to do a better job of living in the present and being thankful for what I have and I could start today with Gran. I let Hemingway out of the room and got ready. When I went downstairs, his big head was lying perfectly contentedly on Gran's lap. She sat there laughing gently, with the warm smile she always seemed to have. I hadn't realized how old she looked, but as she was almost to her eightieth year, I guess it was to be expected. Her face was lined with wrinkles, especially where the smile normally showed. Her hair was completely white and curls were everywhere. Her eyes shone as bright as I ever remembered them. She embraced age well, she really fit the part. Her bony and arthritic fingers gently rubbed down Hemingway's back.

"Morning, Sammy. Sleep well?" she asked through her smile.

"Slept great. Actually did a lot of the thinking," I started before she interrupted.

"You know that thinking always gets you in trouble, dear!" was her warning.

"Oh, I know," I laughed, "but this was good thinking, back to the first several years here in Maine. How crazy they were. Honestly so hard and painful, but so meaningful. I learned more than I ever let myself realize."

"Reflection can be nice. We mustn't dwell there," she offered, "but we can learn there."

We both smiled, knowing how far we had come.

"Let's eat, shall we, dear?" She didn't have to ask twice.

We sat at the table, which had changed a lot, with one space conspicuously empty. Gran had already made pancakes which were being warmed in the oven. As I began to put butter and syrup on mine, I noticed Gran starring out the window, eyes full of tears.

"What'sa matter, Gran?"

She took off her glasses and used her napkin to dab her eyes.

"It's just Ben had been doing so much for me ever since Pops passed," she said, her voice clearly holding back a storm of emotions. "It started slowly, just coming over for company. He knew how hard it was for me when Pops died. But we got really close and as I got less mobile and things got harder, he would take me shopping, help me cook. He really helped me with everything, Sam."

I had no idea about any of the things she mentioned. In hindsight, it seemed every time I had called since Pop's death, he was always there, or had helped her earlier that day. Neither had I realized how tough Pops' death had been. Really, I had allowed myself to become so busy, it was easy to be oblivious to what was happening elsewhere. A mixture of guilt and regret was welling up inside me. I really had not been there at all for anyone the past couple of years. Ben had filled the void I left. I knew now though, that no matter how much I beat myself up over it, nothing could be changed. Gran was starring out the window. I looked, expecting to see a bird dancing on the window sill, but there was nothing.

"You know, we knew he was going to die. We knew he had the cancer."

"No, not at all," I was shocked. "Did he get any treatment? How come no one told me?" The hurt and disappointment had to have been evident in my voice.

"He didn't want anybody to know. Honestly, Sam, just Ben, me and the doctors knew."

"Why didn't he want anyone to know?"

She took a breath. I could tell she was putting the words together in her head.

"Well, I noticed he was losing a lot of weight, but I didn't mention anything to him. He kept complaining of blurred vision and he was really struggling to hear me sometimes. I knew something was up. I kept telling him to go to a doctor, but he said he was fine. There would be times I would look over and see him just doubled up, with really bad headaches. Well, it continued like this for awhile. He began to look sickly and the ladies at the church were always asking me if he was OK. He insisted nothing was wrong, so I went along with his wishes. Finally, about four months ago he was carrying in some groceries for me, and it seemed as though he had been outside for a long time. I went to the door and looked out." Tears were streaming silently from her eyes now. "There he was, just lying there in the yard. He must have collapsed. I called the EMTs and they told me he had had a seizure and lost consciousness. They took him to the hospital and allowed me to ride with him."

I couldn't help but interrupt her, "How come you never told me any of this Gran?" I knew that if I had been more in touch, I would have had to know; it was mostly my fault.

"It'll make more sense, Sam. Let me finish the story." She looked at me, waiting for a response.

"Ok, Gran, I'm sorry, go on," I offered.

"He was unconscious for days. They ran all kinds of tests and did a biopsy. It came back that he had several brain tumors. The cancer had spread pretty much everywhere throughout his body. Well, when he came to, they told him. They gave him the option of surgery and treatment, but they wouldn't guarantee anything. From the very beginning, he refused any type of treatment. At first I didn't understand-- I even got mad at him. But it was his body, his life, and I had to respect his choice and soon I understood. Sam, he was ready to be with his family and fiancée again. He didn't have a death wish, but if death was chasing him, he wasn't going to run. I believe those were his exact words. He just set about preparing to die. He didn't want people feeling sorry for him, or to have to explain to everyone, so he figured no one should know. Obviously, as the days passed, it was clear that he was really sick, but we didn't tell anybody. Eventually, he moved in with me so I could take care of him in his last days when it got really bad. He wasn't afraid at all, Sam. Ben was a brave man. He was so excited to be able to see his family again. As the time dwindled, he told more and more stories about his parents and his beautiful fiancée. Well, the other morning, I came out to make breakfast and I went to check on him and knew he was finally at peace."

"Wow, he died here?" I questioned.

"Yeah, we had a bed put in the living room."

I regretted that was the first thing that came to mind and the only question I asked. We both sat there in silence, clearly thinking over everything. I could tell Gran was really sad, so I figured I'd tell her a story about Ben to cheer her up.

"I remember the last time I saw Ben," I said.

"When was that?"

"Pops' funeral," I admitted.

"Sam, that was seven years ago! It's been that long?"

I regretted that it was so. "Yeah, and I almost didn't make it for that. Remember, back then I was working two jobs, busying myself, trying to pay off school loans. I hardly had time for anything except work, eat and sleep."

"I tried to get you out here," Gran said.

"I know, but not until Pops died could I really put things in perspective. I had regretted the tough choice I made to return to Chicago after graduation. The choice to become a counselor was easy, but moving back to Chicago, a place which meant so much pain and confusion for me was a difficult one. But I busied myself with my work and to me at the moment life was going well. I really did enjoy my job counseling and on top of the forty hours I put in there, I was spending several nights a week loading boxes in a nearby warehouse. Everyone I cared about was in Maine and I struggled with loneliness at times. I promised myself I'd return but never did until it was almost too late."

"I know, Baby," Gran comforted as she took my hand in hers.

I looked out over the sea, took a big gulp of coffee and could almost see Ben out there. It was perfectly tranquil and I could picture him rowing further and further away until he disappeared with that giant smile plastered across his face.

"Tell me more about your last visit, dear," Gran insisted.

"One of the times in life I am most thankful for was the last days I was blessed to spend with Pops before he died. Remember, I had returned home from my job at the warehouse tired and I was worn out from throwing heavy boxes all over the place. I remember it perfectly, the red light on my answering machine was flashing and I almost didn't check the message because I was too tired. But I did and it was Ben on the other end. He told me Loring had had a stroke and that things weren't looking good and he told me to come out."

"That boy never could feel right calling Loring "Pops," could he?" Gran joked.

I smiled, but continued on. "I remember trying to figure out what to do next. I mean it was so sudden and out of the blue, I didn't know how to react. After I called the airport and booked the earliest flight to Portland the next morning, I called Ben and arranged for him to pick me up. That night I didn't catch a minute of sound sleep. The fears of my early years were rushing back to me. I had become so consumed with work and the comfort of my current situation that I was disregarding everyone back in Maine. Things had become exactly the way I had promised those closest to me would never happen, that I would work hard to stay focused on remaining the person I wanted to be. I vividly remember pleading with God, to let me have just a couple minutes with Pops. Never before had I been one to plead like that, but suddenly I had no control, and I felt like I had wasted the last years of Pops' life. Several hours before my flight, I gave up and decided to head to the airport. It was futile to just lie in bed. At the airport I bought a *National Geographic* and read every single article before boarding my flight, but it did little to keep unwanted things off my mind. Finally, I was boarding and ready to fly out. In my mind, I was praying constantly for Pops. I was tired, exhausted from all the worry and I wasn't at all prepared to deal with a situation like this. The flight rolled away from the terminal and soon we were gaining altitude with Chicago shrinking away behind me."

"I know, dear, but you made it. Ben picked you up at the airport and drove you straight to the hospital. We were all there and we were reunited briefly before it was Pops' time. Nothing made Pops happier than to see you one more time and then to die peacefully."

I began to cry. Hearing myself tell that story, I really realized how, after Pops died, I had fallen right back into the same habits. The last moment I shared with Ben in person had been seven years ago when he drove me to the airport for my flight back to Chicago. How had my priorities gotten so skewed over the years? The feeling of failure was beginning to overwhelm me. I would never get to have with Ben the kind of precious last moments I had had with Pops, moments that I treasured so much. It was too late and I had no one to blame but myself. Gran must have noticed me sliding into despair because she quickly changed the subject.

"Well, Sam, you and I are the family today, so get ready to do a lot of greeting and shaking hands, because Ben sure touched a lot of lives." I had never thought about it before but she was absolutely right, we were the closest thing to family Ben had, so it was only right for us to fill that role. "You know, Ben pretty much planned it all with my help before he died," she said with a smile. "Just the viewing tonight and then the funeral tomorrow. They'll transport him back to his hometown where he has a plot next to his beloved fiancée. He didn't even want to have a funeral, but I insisted, and that was one thing he let me have." Then she dropped the bomb on me, "Oh yeah, and he wanted you to do the eulogy."

"Me?" I questioned, "I'm not a pastor or good with words. I figured I would say something but…"

"But that's what he wanted, so you will."

We both knew she was right. We spent the rest of the afternoon looking over Ben's old albums. It was a great time. Gran had seen them, but I had never had a glimpse into Ben's past via pictures. They were to be set out at the viewing, but Gran wanted me to see them first. As I looked through the box of pictures and albums, I noticed one on the table. I knew what it was right away. I picked it up and studied it intently. I'm not sure what the occasion was, but a young Ben was standing there, the brightest and most cheerful I had ever seen him. He had on a navy suit and maroon tie. He had his arm around a beautiful woman with short brown hair. She was absolutely gorgeous and from her expression, she was truly loved. It broke my heart right then and there to look at the picture and see how in love they were. It helped me to get a better understanding of the person Ben had been. On the other side of Ben in the picture were a man and woman who, I assumed, were his parents. His mom was short, with dark hair, and his dad was fit, with a head of grey hair. They were all smiles and all so peaceful. What a wonderful picture, I thought.

Gran walked in with a cup of coffee for me. "Oh, isn't that picture just precious?" She asked.

"Yeah, it's nice to actually see a picture of the people he loved so much. Where did you get it?"

"He brought it with him when he moved in," she explained. "He always kept it by his bed. I would sometimes look in here and he would be sitting holding it, sometimes crying, sometimes laughing, other times, I was sure, he was talking."

"You know what Gran? He should have it," I said as I took it out of the frame, "it only makes sense."

"That's a great idea, Sam."

We gathered everything we would need and left for the funeral home. Parking in back, we walked in the front door and were greeted by the director, an older man with a head which was mostly bald save for some wispy grey hairs. He wore a black suit and a black tie. He took the box full of pictures from us and led us to the room where the viewing would be. On the far side, was the dark wooden casket hidden among flowers that seemed to be from everyone. The casket was half open with white cloths draped around a small man I barely recognized. Without realizing it, I walked up to the casket and had my reunion with Ben. He was forty-four years old now. The cancer had eaten away at him, and his skin was sunken against the bones. He was clean shaven and his hair was short. He had on a grey suit and a navy tie. The tie just seemed to exaggerate how thin his neck and frame now were. His strong muscular structure that I knew so well was now completely gone. His hands were clasped at his waist, thin and bony. But it was still unmistakably Ben. I hadn't expected to, but I began to talk to him.

"I'm sorry Ben, I'm sorry I wasn't here for you through this, I'm sorry I wasn't around after Pops died and I'm sorry that I have to say goodbye when you're already gone." The tears began to build. "But I'm happy for you, I know you've been waiting for this reunion a long time," I finished. I pulled out the beloved picture of him, his parents, and his fiancée and placed it in his jacket pocket.

I felt Gran's hand on my back, "He sure got sickly there at the end, poor Ben."

"Not quite the brawny man he was that first day I worked with him. He never seemed to tire. I could carry bricks to him non-stop."

"People will be here soon," advised the funeral director.

We quickly organized the picture display table. Ben had helped a lot of people, but it seemed like so long ago that as wonderful as he was, I didn't picture too big a turnout. I was shocked by all the flowers, but I assumed that many people had sent flowers and wouldn't to come to the viewing. Fifteen minutes before the scheduled start time, the first family arrived. Not long after that, several more came through the door and that set the pace for the rest of the night. Soon it was so crowded I couldn't tell who was there until they came and talked to Gran and me. Throughout the entire evening, we heard endless stories that were new to us of Ben helping a stranger, or driving to fix a car in the middle of the night, doing work for free, and on and on. It seemed he had made everyone's life better just by being himself. The room was completely filled with people I didn't recognize, some of whom recognized me. I had never really taken the time to make friends during my time in Maine, but Gran knew everyone and their business and spent a lot of the night talking. We would rotate between sitting and standing.

It was during one of Gran's run-on conversations that I looked down the line and was over taken by nerves, my breath was gone and my heart was pumping away. There was no way; it couldn't be her. After she broke my heart, I had done everything I could to avoid her over the years. I had heard she married, but she was here alone tonight. It was Sarah. As much as I hated to admit it she still looked beautiful.

She seemed cheerful and young. She wore a pretty black dress and a solemn expression to match the occasion. In the years since we dated, I had dealt with the pain and emotions, but I had never had to face her. She was slowly working her way to where Gran and I were. I didn't know what to do. When I got a chance I whispered to Gran, "Is that Sarah?"

"Oh yes, she's here, how sweet and brave of her. She's had such a hard time lately."

The phrase made me laugh, but I was embarrassed that I had. She sure taught me a thing or two about a hard time. I tried to control my breathing and focus on the people who were in front of me, but before I could put it off any longer, Sarah was standing before me for the first time in thirteen years.

"Hello, Sam, I'm so sorry about Ben, we all are," she graciously offered me her hand. I accepted and took it in mine. The feel of her hand again after all those years, gave me chills. For a moment I was taken aback; how did she even know Ben? They never met while we were dating.

"How did you know Ben?" The question was too big for me not to ask.

"Well, shoot, it's a long story, Sam. The short version is he really helped me out a lot when my husband left me."

"I'm sorry. I had no idea," I offered.

"You needn't be," she answered. "I'm sorry for everything."

"Well, I think we've all grown up a bit," I smiled.

We hugged and as she walked away, she turned, "You look really nice tonight, by the way."

With that, my mind was a mess, like it hadn't been in years. This was so unexpected. I didn't know what to think. It amazes me how much life can change in a matter of days. A couple days ago was just another day at the office and now I'm back in Maine after seven years and see the ex who broke my heart. How was I supposed to play this one? As I watched her walk away, Gran gave me a nudge.

"Maybe it would be healthy for you two, to catch up," she said, "You're adults now."

"You're right! OK, I'll be right back," I said.

I quickly followed the path I saw Sarah take. She was in the back of the room, looking over the pictures. Reaching out I tapped her shoulder, "Sarah."

"Sam?" She was apparently surprised to see me.

"Yeah, sorry. I was just wondering if, uh, you wanted to catch up, get coffee sometime, I dunno," I said sheepishly.

"That'd be great, Sam," she responded. "What about tonight?"

"You know I'm not in town for long, so that'd be great."

Well, the viewing wound up going an hour over the set time, there was just such a flood and rush of people to see Ben. I was blown away by the entire thing. It made me nervous for the funeral the next day. I still needed to piece my thoughts together for that. After briefly talking with Sarah, we decided I would drop Gran back off at home and then I would meet Sarah at the coffee shop which we knew was open latest, still only giving us 30 minutes or so.

When I arrived there, she had taken the liberty of ordering for both of us; she still knew me, a coffee with cream. The fact that we only had a brief time to catch up forced us to keep the flow moving. It seemed odd to me that someone I once knew more than anyone else and loved so much, was now sitting in front of me as a complete stranger. After the initial small talk and trivialities, Sarah began to describe how she came to know Ben.

"Well, after college, you may have heard I got married that first summer out," she began.

"Yeah, I heard." I said, "To the guy from that day, right?"

Her eyes just looked so sad, as she silently shook her head, "Sam, I'm so sorry, so so sorry."

"Sarah, it's OK, I forgive you. If it wasn't for that, neither Ben nor I would have worked through a lot of issues."

"But still," she continued on, "it's funny we both knew Ben and had no idea."

"You're telling me," I mused.

"Well, like I said, I got married and was married for like five or so years. It was really rocky and never good. He had us move to Camden for his job. The most exhausting five years of my life. Finally he left me completely one day and I realized it needed to end. I needed out. So, I filed for divorce."

"I'm sorry, Sarah …"-- it seemed to be the catch phrase of the night -- "… about all of that. I didn't know you moved to Camden. That definitely passed me."

"Yeah, and I started going to the same church as Ben and Loring and Judith," she explained.

I hadn't heard Pops and Gran called Loring and Judith in quite some time, but things were slowly making more sense. "Did you know who they were, I mean, to me?"

"No, I had no idea, they were really sweet and through some ministries at the church, Ben ended up doing some work for me, mostly fixing things around the house and what not, but he also did my taxes for a couple years. Loring and Judith had me over for lunch a couple times after church."

"No way! I had no idea of this," I interjected.

"Just wait. It gets better," she said slightly laughing. "So the second or third time I was over, I figured I'd get to know them more, so I asked about their family."

"Oh, boy," I said with a smile.

"They raved on and on about their grandson, Sam, who graduated from Bowdoin and moved to Chicago. That's when I knew."

"What'd you do?"

"I told them I graduated from Bowdoin, then I kind of teared up and I was going to say I dated you, but I think they could assume that, with the tears I was fighting."

"Wow, that sounds pretty awkward," I tried to lighten the mood.

"Judith was so sweet. She got up and came over and gave me a big hug. She told me it was all right, and I cried and just said I was sorry." Sarah seemed to stare out the window to avoid eye contact.

I couldn't help it but laugh at the way life played out. This was years ago, too. How come nobody had ever told me, even at Pops' funeral? "How come no one told me?" I questioned.

"Well, they didn't know how you were doing with things and didn't want to reopen old wounds. After the initial shock, it became very comfortable, and we all became regular friends."

"What about Pops' funeral, were you there?"

"No, I was out of town. It broke my heart to miss it, but I had planned another trip with some girl friends of mine from college. Judith insisted I go with them."

"Wait, so you guys are like, good friends?"

Sarah laughed. "No, but she's sweet and at least once a month she tried to have me over for a meal and talked to me at church all the time. It was the same with Ben. It's like they have a sense of when someone is hurting and they go out of their way to make it right, or at least better."

I sat there, looking down at my coffee, twirling the cup and watching as the creamy brown liquid splashed around. Then my eye caught my watch. It was almost closing time. "Oh, shoot, looks like it's about time for us to leave before they kick us out of here."

"Sam, one more thing; I'm sorry if it's weird for you, everything."

"Sarah, it's great. I'm glad you guys are friends. I'm glad you met. They are wonderful people and I love how random life can be. I have peace with all of it," I said with a confident smile.

It had been a great night. I had enjoyed my time with her and was glad Gran had urged me to go. Now I saw, too, that Sarah wasn't free from pain. Sure, she had caused me a lot a long time ago, but that didn't exempt her from her own suffering. Actually, it kind of broke my heart to hear it. There was a time in my life when I would probably have wanted her to get her heart broken; now it just angered me. She seemed so innocent -- but I had thought that once before and it had led me down a wrong path. That made it so much more confusing trying to figure this situation out.

"Well, Sarah, it was a pleasure. I'll see you at the funeral tomorrow. Make sure you say hello," I concluded.

"I'm glad we got to talk, Sam, thanks," she said as she offered a hug.

We got in our cars and drove off. A lot was on my mind as I drove: the events of the night, poor Hemingway cooped up in the house all day and what was I going to say at the funeral tomorrow.

NINE

I couldn't sleep in; in fact, I could barely sleep at all. Around six, I gave up trying and knew what I needed to do. After letting Hemingway out for a brief run, I went to the boat shed and there sat *Santiago*. The years had taken their toll on my beloved vessel. The paint was faded and chipped; I could barely make out the name on the bow. She was covered in dust and looked like she had been in there for a long time. I hadn't rowed in a while, but the sea was calling. Soon I had the old rowboat in the water and had gathered my oars. It seemed to come back quickly for both *Santiago* and me. She cut through the water as well as she ever had and even though I was rusty, we had quite the morning row.

Taking her out to where the house was a distant image and the sea surrounded us, I was able to relax and clear my thoughts to prepare for the day ahead. In my mind, I kept picturing the first time I saw Ben, rowing back from a long day, his now-long-gone beard sprinkled with sea water, sweat on his brow. Now here I was, and no matter how intently I looked, he wasn't going to be in a passing vessel. It came back to me that in my younger days, I would come out and row to escape people and be free from them. It felt as though now I was trying to find someone, someone who was gone. I imagined how much I would like to go out for a row with Pops and Ben. That was something I had never had the chance to do. My arms began to ache; it had been a while since I had rowed and I knew I should be heading in before I wasn't able to row anymore.

I came in and had a nice breakfast with Gran. We talked about Sarah and Gran's take on how all of those events unfolded. Gran shared her side of the story, how she felt as though Sarah had really changed and learned a lot. She had been through a lot of pain and Gran knew nothing else than to just be there for her and love her. It was a pleasant discussion, but before long, I had to excuse myself to go on the porch and collect my thoughts for the eulogy.

Gran had mentioned that Ben had already framed the service and allowed her to tweak it a little bit, so all I had to do was plan what I was going to say. It wasn't that there was any lack of things I wanted to say, but that there was so much I wanted to say that I didn't know how to trim it down to fit in the service. As I sat there and enjoyed the summer morning, my back and arms sore from rowing, an occasional bird would come and perch near me as I wrote and the waves would lap on the shore. They all brought with them images of Ben. They were the things he enjoyed and it seemed as though he was still there with me. I scribbled down some notes and went inside to run them by Gran.

We dressed ourselves up in our finest funeral blacks and were on our way. The day was brilliant, the sun was out and shinning everywhere. The sky was the most inviting blue I had ever seen. I almost felt guilty being sad on such a beautiful day, but as much as I tried, it was hard to forgive myself for my absence over the past several years. Everything seemed a bit surreal and almost dream-like. I wondered how my mother was doing back in Chicago. There were times I tried to excuse my absence from Maine and my loved ones here by saying to myself that she needed me there, but the argument didn't really hold water. I could never really pinpoint why I didn't go and visit. It crossed my mind on numerous occasions, but it was always one of those things I would do next year, which turned into the next year.

As it was, only death would bring me back, and we were arriving at the funeral home. The room was now completely filled with chairs, more chairs than I imagine the fire marshal would be pleased with. But after the viewing, I think we all knew the numbers would be necessary. We went over the details and made sure everything was ready and then we waited. Slowly people trickled in. Old friends from church, Sarah, different people from Camden and the surrounding areas all came to say goodbye to our mutual friend. As they arrived, the seats filled slowly and the director was frantically adding chairs here and there where there was space. And then there was a scene that would have made Ben proud. Men began getting up and offering their seats to ladies and children and went to stand in the back and in the doorway. By the time we were ready to begin, there wasn't an empty chair in the room and the sides and the back were filled with men and some wives standing. The scene in itself was enough to portray the impact Ben's life had on all of us. Thinking to myself how much pain I knew he carried and was burdened with, he nevertheless had made many people's lives better. It was truly inspiring.

I led Gran to the podium to begin the funeral. "I'd like to thank all of you for being here today to say goodbye

to our good friend, Benjamin Stockbridge, or as many of us knew him, simply 'Ben.'" As she spoke I could hear the age in her voice. It was as strong as ever but there was clearly an older sound to it. She wore the same black dress that she had worn at Pops' funeral and the pearl necklace Pops had gotten her for their tenth anniversary, with pearl earrings he got her to celebrate my college graduation. Pops always loved pearls because they were from the sea, and he had a fascination with the sea. "It seems tragic for someone so young to be taken from us, yet I know no one more prepared for death. It wasn't that Ben had a death wish, he just knew what was waiting on the other side. Ben moved to Maine almost twenty years ago. I met him at church and immediately was very fond of him. As many people here know, he would do anything for anyone, no matter what the sacrifice was on his own behalf. He grew close to Loring and me, and our grandson, Sam, so close that he became part of our family, a new son."

She fought back tears as she spoke of a new son, knowing there still hadn't been a single word on the whereabouts of her real son, my father, since the news of my mother's pregnancy. But I think Ben did something special to fill that void and heal that pain in her life. "That is why today I say goodbye to him as a son. I am privileged to say I got to spend almost the same amount of time with Ben as his real mother, yet that also breaks my heart. Knowing the man that Ben was, it is easy for us understand the magnitude and character of his parents' love when they were taken from him so tragically at age twenty-two. Ben was well versed in loss throughout his life, and yes, he struggled with it, but he never allowed it to interfere with helping others. As I look out over this audience, I know without a doubt that every single person here can honestly say their life is better for having known Ben."

She looked up and her eyes were met with a chorus of nodding heads and the occasionally uttered,"that's right," or "yes."

"Ben knew death was near and was able to plan this service himself. He picked out the songs and the order, but I made him add a part or two. What he truly intended was that this would be a celebration of life and the lives of all of us, not a mournful weeping at his death, but a joyous celebration at all the life we share together. Would you join me in singing one of his favorite hymns, "It is Well with My Soul."

The congregation all began on Gran's lead, "When peace like a river attendeth my way…" As we sang, I was taken back to the first service many years ago, when I saw Ben singing this song from deep within. That image never left me over the years. Back then, I wasn't as fond of the song, but through my trials and experiences I grew to love it similarly and could still close my eyes and see him belting it out as his beard exaggerated his words, the chaos of pain, hope, and joy in his eyes. Something I could never forget. The thought brought tears to my eyes, but I could honestly stand witness that "…it was well with my soul."

As the song ended, Gran introduced the next part of the service, "This next part Ben didn't want included, but I insisted and he said, 'Well, as long as I am dead, you can go ahead with it.'" She paused, hoping for some laughs, which she got. "But in all honesty I know many of you out here would love to share what Ben has done for you, a story or anything, so for this next part just come and share."

Immediately, a line began to form. I wasn't sure who the first man was. He was elderly, looked to be older than Gran, and he was dressed in an old pressed suit, with his tie split and going in two directions. Taking out a handkerchief, he wiped his mouth and cleared his throat: "Hello there. My name is Otis, I don't know many of you, but I knew Ben. You see, we were members of AA together. After my wife died from cancer, I turned to drinking and I would be drunk all day, every day. Finally, my daughter convinced me to go to AA at the church and there I met Ben. He shared his story and he was there for me, encouraging me, supporting me and full of understanding…" Otis broke down and had to wait for the tears to pass. "But thanks to be to God, because of Ben, I can say I'm four years sober." Turning to Ben in the casket, I saw him whisper, "Thank you, Ben."

Next was a younger family from the church. They got up and told the story of their husband and father losing his job just before a real bad storm did severe damage to their roof. Ben had a group of men come by and fix the roof for free. Several old ladies told stories of Ben taking them shopping, to the senior center, to church. It seemed from the stories, he almost had a taxi service for the elderly ladies of the church. Many of them told stories of his fixing things around the house, whether it be the air filter or redoing an entire room. Another man told a story of Ben giving him a job and allowing him to work with him after he got out of prison and couldn't get work anywhere else. Sarah got up and told the story of how Ben had been there for her and supported her through her husband's leaving. After she spoke, she looked over to me, smiled, and an old familiar chill ran down my spine.

Mrs. Holt was next. I knew her story, which was similar to Ben's but many years down the road. Her words were forced out through tears, "Ben and I had similar stories. You see, my husband and daughter were killed in a car accident some twenty years ago. At the funeral, this young man I had never seen before came up to me, telling me he had read in the paper about what happened and wanted to say he understood how I felt and he gave me the best hug I can ever remember. That man was Ben. I was almost mad at him at first because he could be so young and be doing so well with his pain, but then I realized he wasn't, he was still hurting and grieving, and he gave me space to do the same. We would get together and weep and share stories, and from this grew the grief support group at church I know many of you have been to. I would just like to say thank you, Ben. Enjoy your reunion and tell my dear Bob and little Clarissa I miss them and am looking forward to our reunion as well."

As the stories spilled out -- and, boy, did they! -- it seemed as though everyone took a turn to say something. I soon recognized a common theme: Ben never once asked for anything in return or even expected it. He just did what he did because he believed it was right.

It was almost overwhelming to see how many lives he had touched. It would be hard to follow all these tremendous stories. But they were good for the soul. Reading all the bad news in the paper and hearing negative reports from many other sources can be overwhelming, and the hope one good man can offer can change your entire perspective. That's what most people in that room needed at one point or another, simply hope, and that's what Ben had given them.

Once everyone had a chance to speak and tell their story or just say goodbye, Gran came back and started the next song, Ben's most favorite hymn, "Come Thou Fount of Every Blessing." Once again, the room was taken away in a chorus of voices. It was good to hear this song and know that he was receiving the blessing he had been waiting for so long. He was reunited. As the song came to a close, I got up and took the podium in my hands.

"Hello. I know a lot of you out there today, but some of us are strangers. I'm Samuel Slade, Judith's grandson," I said with a wink to Gran, "…and Ben was my best friend. When I was thinking of what to share today, I wrote down a lot of thoughts. But as Gran," I laughed, "or as most of you know her, Judith, was speaking earlier, I couldn't help but notice her pearls. I say that because Ben's life really reminds me of a pearl, the great suffering and pain early on in his life made the latter part of his life the pearl we are all here to celebrate. I feel as though when Ben saw others suffering he worked to turn their pain into a pearl we, in turn, could use to inspire others. And I'm thankful for that. In my younger days I met Ben, and he was there for me through very difficult, painful times in my past. One such event caused me to get in a great fight with him. He was trying to change my pain into a pearl, but I wouldn't have any of it. That happened the summer after my freshmen year of college, but as I thought about his words and read the letters he wrote me almost monthly after that, I really progressed and I was able to deal with not only that particular pain but a great deal of other pain from my past.

"Finally, after my college graduation, Ben and I went for a walk along the coast. We both knew there was a lot that needed to be said. I asked forgiveness and told him that he had changed my life and that I was sorry I had to cause him pain to do so. But he wouldn't have any of it. He told me that I had changed his life and helped him realize he still had changes to be made. I don't know about that, but I know even in moments like that, Ben would never blame me for anything. Ben said he knew risks when he took them. He opened himself to love me and in doing so, I caused him pain, but that didn't cause him to shy away from staying open to that love. Luckily, he did because we grew from that and became even closer friends than we had been before. His love for his parents and his fiancée were so great, he carried that pain with him daily. I don't know why I tell this story, but for an example of Ben's selflessness and great capacity for love."

I paused to collect my thoughts. Why had I shared that thought? I wasn't sure. I was sweating and nervous. I guess I was so eager to give a eulogy worthy of Ben or maybe I was just embarrassed, I don't know. But an encouraging nod from Gran and I continued on. "When I've been trying to come to peace with Ben's sudden passing, there is one image I like to cling to: I close my eyes and I see a celestial shore, the beach is lined with beautiful pebbles, all different sorts of faded blues, grassy greens, dark chocolate browns, and they don't hurt to walk on. The gentle waves roll down with each rhythm singing out their rocky chorus. On the outskirts of the shore are pines, giant pines reaching into heaven. Out walks a fair maiden, Ben's maiden, his beloved fiancée because she knows his time is near, and she is dressed in the most magnificent wedding gown, adorned more beautifully than the most beautiful nighttime sky with stars out in full force. She waits patiently as something breaks in the distance. It's a man and he's rowing. It's Ben. He's smiling, but his rowing remains constant, he knows that will get him there faster than being frantic. They both are smiling and anxious. Ben cuts through the crystal waves. He is dressed in a brilliant suit fit for the king of grooms. He nears and the anticipation grows, all the pain of waiting and separation suddenly seems so worth it because the glorious reunion is here. Before he gets to shore he drops the oars and turns to his fiancée, with a great leap he jumps out of the boat and sprints toward her, his speed constantly building. At first she just stands there, but the joy overwhelms her and she picks up the train of her dress and runs towards Ben. Finally they meet and embrace, his strong arms wrapping her up and showering her with kisses and affirmation as joy radiates from the two. They are together again and will never have to part."

I pause after that story, feeling better, and a feeling of warmth comes over me, almost as though I was the one being embraced. "One day we will join them and we will celebrate with them, but for now we must do as Ben did for so many years and carry on in this world. We must work to carry on his legacy and make life better for others. For one day, our time will come and we will share in our very own reunions, but it is not this day for us. As the years pass by, the thought of the spirit land where Ben and his family and so many loved ones of ours dwell will no doubt grow and become more and more heavenly. Ben, I love you, and you saved my life."

As I walked down I turned for a moment to the casket. I'm not sure why, but a smile came across my face and I felt joyous. Ben was free. Gran came back and dismissed everyone to head to the church for the reception. Since Ben was being buried in his hometown in Ohio on his plot with his fiancée, I would accompany the body and be there for the burial. We would leave the next day. Until then we had the reception and getting the most out of my time with Gran. Once everyone was cleared out, the funeral director gave Gran and me one last moment with Ben before he closed the casket. We each said our final goodbye in our own way. Then we were off to enjoy the fellowship waiting at church. We got our food and sat down at a table next to Sarah. Several of Gran's friends joined us as well. I sat trying to figure out whether I had subconsciously or purposely sat down next to Sarah. It seemed I was still suffering from my old case of over-thinking everything.

Sarah said, "That was a beautiful picture you gave us, Sam. Thank you."

"I agree. How sweet, dear. Brought tears to my eyes," offered one of Gran's friends.

"Thank you, ladies, I've pictured that over and over again since I found out, and every time I just get happy for Ben."

"He was something else; we were all lucky to know him," Gran said.

As we enjoyed the array of food, we were all dealing with mixed emotions. As we talked, we realized that we all were so happy for Ben, as funny as it sounded to say. It brought us happiness to know he was reunited with his beloved and his parents even though we were going to miss him. We would miss his smile, his infectious laugh, and his understanding nod.

"A lot of people are going to have to step up to take his place," another one of Gran's friends insisted.

"Or us old ladies will never get groceries," Gran said, as they all erupted in laughter.

As I sat there during conversation, I had no idea what to do with regard to two matters. First, Gran. I hated to leave her out in Maine all alone, but I knew she would never move away. I also knew she was too old to be able to take care of herself without someone like Ben or me nearby, and that broke my heart. Then, to keep things all confused, there was Sarah. I felt like I was attached to her and I didn't know why I was fighting those feelings. I mean, I was thirty-two years old now. Shouldn't I be beyond that?

After the meal, they insisted Gran and I not help with clean up. We said our goodbyes, and I arranged to have breakfast with Sarah the next day before I left and we returned home.

"What a day, Sam, what a day," said Gran.

"What a week, heck, what a life," I laughed.

Hemingway was eager to have company again and was bounding between the two of us to see who would offer the most rubs. Finding Gran more patient, he made the smarter choice and finally settled with her. I put some coffee on and once again it was just Gran and me alone with our thoughts. I wasn't sure how best to say it so I just came right out. "Gran I think you should move to Chicago with me. Now, let me get my thoughts out before you object, all right?"

"I disagree completely, but I'll let you talk, if it makes you feel better," she said with a wink.

"Now that Ben is gone, there won't be anyone here to take care of you and make sure you're all right, Gran. If you move to Chicago, you can live with mom and me and we -- well, I -- can take care of you. You'll like Chicago." Now I was lying through my teeth. As soon as those words came out of my mouth, I knew it and I knew she would never be happy there. The look on her face said it all. No matter what I said, she would not move away from Maine. She would get by and I knew she could.

"Maybe you should move back here, did you ever think about that, Sam?"

"No, honestly, the thought hadn't crossed my mind. What about my mom, and my job and all my commitments in Chicago, my patients?"

"That's life Sam. If you stay because of your patients, you'll always get new ones and you'll be there forever. Your mom can come back here; it would do her good to be back. We could help her. It's just a thought, Sam. You could fix up *Santiago*, you could find patients here. I just think maybe you'd be happier. There's also Sarah. Who knows what could come of that? Maybe your timing was wrong, maybe it's finally right?"

We were both silent, neither one in agreement with each other. "I'm sorry Sam, I guess when you started telling me what to do, I just had to one up you." She said it gently with a smile.

"Who knows what will happen, Gran? Promise me you'll think about it, and I'll think about what you said. I have a long drive tomorrow, which will be a lot of time to think. How does that sound?"

"That should be good. Now, let's drink that coffee."

We sipped our coffee, and I thought about how much I would love to refurbish *Santiago*. To see a fresh coat of paint on her old sides would be so refreshing. To take her out again daily as though I was a teen again was exciting to think about. Thinking of *Santiago* brought back thoughts of Pops. I surely missed him. That was a reunion I was looking forward to. I decided I wanted to go to his grave before I left town.

"Hey, Gran, I was thinking of going over to Pops' grave. Would you like to join me?"

"Ben used to take me there all the time. I'd like to."

So, we got ready and drove off to the cemetery. We walked through the rows until we came to his name, Loring Slade, seemingly so alone in the row of graves. There was the plot where Gran would be laid to rest one day, but for now it seemed to be a lonely arrangement. It made me wonder, when I die, if I would be buried alone. The thought was sad to me. I was happy Ben would be laid to rest with his fiancée, and Gran and Pops had each other, but where did that leave me? I pictured my lonely grave marker on the side of a hill in the cemetery, all alone. The thought sent an eerie chill through my body. It seemed such a lonely fate, but I realized sitting there, looking at Pops' grave, that I wasn't alone. I was one in a long line of Slades and I could honestly be proud to call myself that. In my younger days, I had hated it more than anything, but Pops really taught me to be proud of my heritage and be proud of who I was. One bad Slade didn't ruin the rest and as mad as I had been at my father, I counted myself in the good company of many Slades, just not him. I still looked through the old family album Pops had made me in those lost days and it gave me great encouragement.

I decided to walk the rows to think for awhile, while Gran stayed by Pops' grave. I knew she missed him and I knew in a strange way, Ben's death gave her encouragement to understand that in due time it would come and they would have their own reunion. It was still a struggle for her until then. I was glad it wasn't her time yet, though. I still had a lot to learn from her. While I had come a long way in my life and learned so much from Pops, Gran and Ben, I knew I still had a long way to go. I returned and sat with Gran at Pops' grave, putting my arm around her as we watched the sun set over the hill. Then we walked back to the car. The drive home was dark and the stars filled the void like salt spilled on a marble counter. I loved the Maine night. It was so quiet and calm. When we got home, I packed my things and stayed up a little later than usual to talk to Gran. We talked for a long time and it was nice to be able to share my fears and insecurities about the future and lessons I felt I had learned over the short visit. I couldn't believe that it was already time for me to be returning, but Gran and I were able to plan a good arrangement for the future.

We reached an agreement that pleased us both very much. With that I went to be bed, knowing tomorrow would be a long day. I didn't want to fall asleep; I knew that would mean tomorrow and that would mean leaving. Trying to stay up like a child waiting on Santa Claus, I kept going back to stories that I remembered from years past. I was trying to remember my favorite times with Ben, especially. A certain memory I hadn't reflected on about in years came to mind. It was right after graduation when I was contemplating going back to live in Chicago. I didn't really want to leave Maine, but I felt as though I needed to be in Chicago to restore things with my mother. I had come along far enough to be able to forgive her and needed to do it in person and be there for her as she never was for me. I felt that very strongly, but it would mean I would have to leave Maine, and all that included: Pops, Gran, and Ben, with whom I had also restored my relationship.

Ben had a conversation with me, about following your heart. He sat there, looked me in the eyes and said words I've never forgotten. "If you feel something in your heart, Sam, you mustn't fight it. You must embrace it, chase it and work toward it. Yes, it will call for sacrifice; no great things in life are without them, but in the end you'll be glad you did." It was the encouragement I needed, but it still didn't bring complete peace until he finished with this thought, "…and just because you are called somewhere now, doesn't mean you might not be called back later." At the time I had no idea what he meant by that. I don't even know if he did. But I had never forgotten those words, I even wrote them down. Now they seemed very prophetic and true.

I was glad I had gone to Chicago. It had taken time, endless patience and a lot of work but I was able to restore my relationship with my mom. The years had taken their toll and she was full of regret, sorrow, and loneliness. The stepfather I had hated so much had left her and she had been left all alone to dwell in her mistakes. But through my unconditionally forgiving her, she was able to learn to forgive herself.

We became regular parts of each other's lives and made up for lost time. I wished as I lay there, that I could have one last conversation with Ben on what to do next in life, just what step to take. But I knew the wish was futile and soon I was asleep.

When I woke up, Gran was up, ready to say goodbye, first to Hemingway, and then to me. We hugged and I kissed the top of her head, "I love you Gran. I'm glad we figured everything out."

"I love you, too, Sam. Let me know how today goes and be safe."

As I drove away, she stood there, all alone in the doorway, waving goodbye. It was so hard to drive away but I knew I must. I knew for both of our sakes, I had to continue on. Luckily, I had breakfast with Sarah to keep me from dwelling on those thoughts. It would have to be a brief breakfast since I had to meet the funeral director. We both ordered coffee, I had a blueberry muffin and she chose a chocolate chip. I remarked, "Some things never change."

"Yet, so much changes," she responded and was she ever right.

"Do you remember what book you were reading when we first met?" I regretted asking as soon as I did, fearing it would look odd that I remembered after all these years. She sat there clearly thinking, and obviously frustrated.

"I don't even have a guess, isn't that horrible?"

"I think it's worse that I remember," I said with a laugh, trying to cover up. "It was *The Count of Monte Cristo*. I remember because I went out and bought *The Hunchback of Notre Dame*. Just so you would think our interests were the same. How young and foolish I was."

"Aw, that's so cute, Sam, what a little romantic," she teased.

"Well, if we back then could see us sitting here now, I think we'd be very confused." It made hardly any sense to me; I had a tendency to ramble on about useless things when I was around Sarah.

"As confusing as that actually sounded, it makes sense to me," she confessed.

It was true. I had no doubt I would marry her and be with her forever, but right then, she seemed more like a stranger to me than a former love. But there was a level of excitement with that. It just meant there were new things to find out and discover about each other. It was exciting and scary all at the same time, but I wouldn't allow myself to decide what I really thought about the matter. I knew if I allowed myself, I would get lost forever in my thoughts and not spend a single moment in reality so I fought to get back to what matters. As we sat there reminiscing over breakfast, I admitted that I was glad that we had gotten back in touch.

"You know, getting reunited has been a pleasant surprise, Sarah. I really never thought I would ever see you again and now here we are. I'm glad we have been able to spend the amount of time together we have." I couldn't believe I was being so honest and open with her. It seemed to come easy and that really scared me. What I didn't share with her was this: I figured if anything was meant to happen, I would let it fall into place and not force it as I had so many years ago. It might work out better for me in the end. I would take my hands off and not be active and just let what would be, simply be. We both talked a little bit of nonsense as the time flew by. Before I knew it I needed to be on the road. "Well, Sarah, I'm afraid our time must end for now, I have to be on my way."

"I guess you're right. It's a shame we can't waste a whole day."

She was right. I would have loved to spend a whole day getting to know each other and catching up, but it wasn't meant to be; if it was, I believed, it would have happened. But I was minutes away from leaving and it clearly wasn't in the cards. We hugged and I said another goodbye in what seemed to be a stream of endless goodbyes and then drove to the funeral home to meet the director and head out on my final goodbye.

TEN

I met the funeral director outside the funeral home. He was eager for the drive.

"I feel like a limo driver, driving someone to pick up their prom date," he confessed. As much of a stretch as that was, I knew what he meant. Really, the task of reuniting the old lovers was his. We were both honored to be the chosen ones and glad for it to finally happen. So, leaving from the funeral home, I followed the hearse from Camden to central Ohio, where Ben's fiancée was buried. Unfortunately the drive felt like slow motion. It seemed the closer we got to our destination, the slower time went.

Things seemed to not go right; there were always commercials on the radio and I couldn't get the right temperature in the car. The scenery was constantly changing, but the car in front never changed. That in itself presented too much time to think about Ben being in a casket in the back of the car. The frailty of life really struck me: A man as capable and strong as Ben met the same end as everyone else. No one can avoid it. We all end up in the back of a hearse. When I reflected on my own thoughts, I realized that following the hearse for so long had caused them to turn rather morbid and I was slightly disturbed by this. So, it was a very welcome change when we stopped for lunch at a small restaurant in Pennsylvania. The funeral director chose the spot. He told me he liked to try little quaint and homely places because sometimes you find the best food there. We gave this place a shot; the waitress was friendly and eager to serve, but the food was far from hitting the spot. I told him I hated to admit it but this time he was wrong. Luckily he was so wrong, he admitted it himself. We had a good laugh and we each got a coffee to drink. Back in the car, even Hemingway's dog food in the backseat looked appealing.

As we continued on our journey, my thoughts turned back to the more cheerful aspects of life and the joys of the trip I had experienced. I was growing weary from the drive but I knew we were close to our destination. By the time we arrived, it was very late and I checked in a hotel for the night. We would bury him early the next morning and then I would drive the rest of the way to Chicago. I had planned on going to the cemetery to see the plot, but by the time we arrived it was dark and I decided the better of it. I took Hemingway for a long walk, followed by a relaxing shower and then I settled into a good book. I hadn't allowed myself enough time to read lately. In the past I was an avid reader, but lately, all I had time for was the paper and email. Luckily this thought had hit me before we left Maine and I had snuck some old favorites from the house when we left. Looking in my bag, I selected one and I opened up Hawthorne's *The Scarlet Letter*, and allowed myself to be taken away to the world of the book much as I had in my high school days when I fell in love with reading for the first time. Anytime you go without something you enjoy for a while, when you get back to it, it is new and wondrous again. I fought hard against the sleepiness I felt beginning to overwhelm me, but soon I was asleep.

With the morning sun, I was once again dressed for a funeral which seemed to be a regular happening as of late. Meeting with the funeral director, we drove to the cemetery. Walking down the rows, I came across it. I had long imagined it but it was a lot different that I had pictured. Finally, there was her gravestone, plain yet beautiful, just her name under which was simply phrased, "Beloved fiancée, we will meet again." Thinking of her and Ben's story reminded me of a poem, I had once read in college, "Ode on a Grecian Urn." In it, John Keats speaks of these two figures, "never can thou kiss", forever suspended so close, yet impossible to join. It seemed Ben had to live that out for many years, but now the figures finally overcame the impossible and I pictured Ben and his fiancée as two figures on a Grecian urn, in their death coming to life and finally kissing and that image now the final image on the urn forever. Next to her stone was his stone, Benjamin Stockbridge, and his also read, "Beloved fiancé, we will meet again." The stones were very different than I had pictured, but Ben was a simple man with great love, and he didn't need a great monument to that love. Really, just being there was an experience. It felt powerful to be here in this place for their earthly reunion. While I knew their souls were far off, it brought tears to my eyes to be able to witness the reunion of their bodies. It felt as though there was a peace in the universe that I didn't even recognize was missing.

I decided that it was better to love like them, so tragically and so painfully than to not love at all. Love was too great a thing to pass up and I had spent so many years of my life doing just that. Running from love--I guess I could say sometimes even rowing from it. Yes, I had been hurt, but standing there at the grave of two lovers of the most tragic sort, I realized that I needed to open up again, I needed to risk. I needed to be more like Ben. Maybe his final lesson to me was to come from the grave, but it was time for me to live again. The prospect filled me with excitement. It was like a new birth a second chance at life. The day was warm and the air was fresh. Robins fluttered on a nearby tree and a pond not far off in the cemetery was the playground for a family of ducks.

The funeral director wanted to say a prayer, "Father, Mighty God, for years I have tended your flock on their final passage from this life to true life. I thank you for this beloved soul which is now in paradise with you. May you bring fulfillment to his incomplete dreams and hopes from this life and may we live in the way he did to affect others. Above all your will be done. In your name, Amen."

He asked me to say some words, I had nothing prepared so I spoke from the heart, "Ben, your body is finally home, yet your soul is finally free. You taught us how to live and to find the pearls in life. I am so thankful that I was able to be your friend. Enjoy yourself, dance with your fiancée, and be on the lookout: One day I'll row up on those very same shores."

It wasn't much, but they were the words that came to my heart. The cemetery staff would lower the casket, so our work was done. As I parted ways with the funeral director, I felt as though a chapter of my life was being closed. I hadn't really thought about it that way before, but it was the end of one era, which meant the beginning of a new one. It was up to me to live in such a way that I could at least touch one life the way Ben had touched the many who had been there to say their goodbyes. If I tried to compare my life to Ben's, I knew I would never be satisfied, but I knew if I used his life as an example and tried to touch just one life as he had touched so many, I would be able to say I was successful.

Hemingway and I took a long walk partly for his exercise and partly for the well being of my mind. I couldn't believe how fast the time in Maine had gone and that in a matter of hours I would be back to the grind in Chicago. I was torn over trying to make the trip last and taking my time and getting home and bringing it to an end sooner rather than later. I asked Hemingway, "Should we go or stay?" He must have understood enough because he pointed off in the opposite direction of the car. "Yeah, I'm not ready to leave yet either."

So we didn't, we just lingered. I knew Ben's parents were in another plot at the same cemetery so we walked around until we came to theirs. They shared a stone with the inscription, "We lived full of love and left this world together, hand in hand." I knew those were Ben's words. He had told me it brought him great peace that his parents were able to enter heaven together. We lingered there momentarily paying our respects to the parents who had raised such a magnificent

172

son in such a short span. Not familiar with the area, we didn't go anywhere else, but we didn't go home either, not yet. We just stayed, almost soaking in the remnant of time, thinking back through the lessons and wondering what the next chapter would bring. But I knew as all good things I couldn't linger forever, the next page had to come, so finally when we were both ready, Hemingway and I got back in the car and made the tireless journey mostly through endless cornfields with a stretch of windmills back to Chicago.

We arrived late at night. Once again, my house seemed so empty and lonely. I had Hemingway but I missed Gran, I had been spoiled. It also meant it was once again up to me to fix meals, but feeling lazy and not up to cooking I ordered a pizza. What I really craved was some of Gran's New England clam chowder. As I waited for the delivery, I turned on the TV, flipping through all of the channels nothing caught my interest and soon I turned it off, preferring instead to take out my book and continue reading the great story Hawthorne was spreading out before me. As I looked up from the page, it seemed even Hemingway didn't feel right being at home. He sat with his head hanging off the couch, lethargic. I opened the door to let him out back and he just lay there. I knew how he felt. The pizza came and I ate alone as I had so many times before, but this time it was actually lonely. After dinner I went back to reading but all I really wanted was to go to sleep and wake up back in my bed in Maine.

It was funny how much things had changed over such a short period of time. It wasn't long ago I wouldn't go there for anything, not even with my loved ones there, and now I wanted nothing more. I wanted to make coffee but I knew that I needed my sleep. I went out on the porch to look up at the stars. They were out but seemed so faint and few compared to the brilliant night sky of Maine. I struggled with my thoughts. I had to admit as I considered my present circumstances little bit of fear grew inside me; I wondered if I was chasing some fantasy that wouldn't be real. Say, I did return, even move there, would it be like the time was the past week, or would it become routine and as stagnant as Chicago had become for me. Or was that just another excuse to not move there? And what about Sarah? Should I pursue her? I had so many questions, it seemed I had a plague of unanswered questions.

Suddenly I laughed because deep down inside a longing I hadn't felt in years was growing and I tried to suppress it but it was no use. Finally, it spilled out: I longed to be in *Santiago*, my arms aching once again from rowing, while the shore faded on the horizon. To sit with my back to the sea as I watched my worries disappear in front of me. To feel the keel cutting through the surf as the waves breaking splashed coolly on my skin. To look up and to see a bird flying high above and be as free as he, or see a fish break the surface and know we were comrades. Free from worries and questions, alone with the sea once again. The place I knew so well from my dreams of old had suddenly found its way back to me. Shaking my head I stood up and looked out over my little fenced-in backyard. I had to remind myself that I was no longer in Maine and to drop my little fantasy because it wasn't an option. Knowing I had work the next day, I decided sleep was the best option. I would rest and tomorrow would be a new day, fresh thoughts and maybe a little clarity on my situation.

As I lay in bed, fighting to fall asleep I had little luck. There was simply too much on my mind. The events seemed surreal and now all I could do was to analyze every detail and rethink every moment. I think deep down inside I knew what I had to do, but I was working to convince myself of it when I finally feel asleep. I don't remember the moment, but I knew I was asleep when I am back in Maine. I remember thinking "This is it!" But I must be dreaming. I am on a porch, much like Gran's but older. I can't see myself, but I can feel a long white beard. I assume I have become an old man. I feel happy and content. The sun is out and shines brightly on the water. The trees are all green and dark orange needles lie everywhere on the ground. Everything is new to me, yet so familiar as if I have been there a thousand times. Sitting there, I gently rock back and forth in my chair while my mind is at peace. Finally I am not lonely, for I have love in my life, whoever it is, sits there in the chair next to me. Try as I might I can't quite make out who, but I feel affection and love for and from whomever it is. I am happy, genuinely happy. Feelings I have been chasing and running from for years have all arranged themselves for this perfect moment. My love's hand is in mine and it feels as though we are waiting for the sun to set and enjoying every moment until it does. Finally it sets with the most brilliant moment right before the final glimpse of light, when everything is illuminated and the colors stand at their truest. Everything is calm but when the sun finally sets, it is all gone.

My alarm startled me awake. But the questions and apprehensions from the night before were all gone. The peace from my dream had remained and I knew exactly what I was going to do. I went downstairs and decided to celebrate by making a wonderful breakfast. Scrambled eggs, bacon, buttered toast, and nothing for me was ever complete without a cup of coffee and cream.

First , I called my mom and shared with her the entire experience and all of my thoughts. She was very open and in agreement, her poor mental health wasn't nearly up to par and I knew she needed me so that was pivotal to my decision. I'm not sure if she was still feeling the need to make up for poor decisions in my past or if she was really was as supportive of the idea as I, but she completely agreed and that was what mattered. Next I called Gran and talked it over with her. She was excited and eager, and listened patiently as I explained it all. Finally when I hung up I sat there at the table eating and I wrote out a letter, not a letter I would send, but one I would hand deliver that very day. It was a freeing and liberating experience. The words came easily and I knew it was right. I put it in an envelope in my briefcase as I walked out the door wishing goodbye to Hemingway in the backyard.

I missed the endless pines from Maine as I drove to work past endless houses, stores, and businesses. Small ponds in developments didn't represent even a vestige of the real sea. I knew this wasn't home. I arrived at work and walked in. The receptionist asked how my trip was, and I said it was wonderful and that I had come to a lot of realizations while I was gone. Seeing she wasn't interested in my answer, I walked through to my office. Checking my appointments for the day, my first was with a young boy who had lost both his parents. We had made tremendous progress and this was our last official day. It gave me great hope and I felt better about myself for being able to help at least this one person. I was eager to for our session that day and was pleased when he arrived early. When our time was up, I was proud of his saying goodbye and I knew I was making the right decision. I walked out the door and back to the receptionist and taking out the letter I had written at breakfast, I asked her to deliver it to my boss. With a quizzical look she said she would.

Stopping to refill my coffee, I took my time going back to the office. I decided to go for a brief walk and the receptionist was clearly at a loss when I walked right out the front door. Walking around the building, I went to a bench by the jungle gym. Today it was sunny and the cloudy blue sky warmed my face. The usual mothers were at the park with their young children. The jungle gym was full, little boys seemed to be having a contest on the monkey bars struggling not to lose their grips as two little girls took turns pushing each other on the swings. Several kids were playing tag and running around without a care in the world. The puddles that had formed the day I left were now completely dried up. I sat there taking it all in. I closed my eyes and just listened to the laughter and shouts as they rang up in a chorus so free. I loved the innocence of a child's laugh, so carefree and genuine. It seemed things were so much more simple at that age. We adults seemed to complicate life so much, I guess it is inescapable in a way, but it seemed tragic to me. I watched a bird flying high above, riding the currents of the wind, and angling to stay in flight. The trees stood strong and steadfast and full of life. Squirrels anxiously ran up and down their trunks, pausing with every noise. I couldn't help but smile; it truly was a beautiful day. Finishing the last of my coffee, I gathered myself and headed back inside. Smiling at the receptionist, just to add to her confusion, I continued through to my office.

Sitting down at my desk I noticed the flashing red light on my phone. Not eager to push it, I took the old Slade Family Album out of my top desk drawer. I sat there going through every page of history. What a wonderful keepsake it was. It was hard for me to remember what I was like to be so ashamed of the family I came from, back when I knew so little. I had looked through that album endless times and it never grew old. I turned my attention to the answering machine, staring contently, not knowing what waited for me at the click of the button. Watching the red light alternate between off and on reminded me of the lighthouses I loved so much in Maine. I felt like a child contented to stare at the flashing light. I was startled back into reality with an actual ring on the phone.

"Hello, this is Sam Slade," I answered.

"Sam, what in the world happened to you over that trip?" It was my boss; he must have read my letter. "We need to talk about this and make sure you are making the right choice."

"I had a lot of revelations and I'm sure it's the right choice, I've had plenty of time to think it over myself," I assured him.

"Well, I value you, Sam, and your judgment so I'll support any decision you make, but I would like to talk it over with you just to help clarify the decision for both our sakes; how does lunch today sound?"

"I can do that, sounds good."

I hung up the phone and I had to admit it was quite liberating. I breathed out a sigh of relief, it really seemed the pieces were falling into place and I was beginning to get the reassurance I needed, the reassurance that I thought could only come through a conversation with Ben. My attention was drawn back to the answering machine. I had assumed the message was from my boss, but now I knew it wasn't. Reaching out I went ahead and hit the button, "You have one unheard message, first unheard message," the ever familiar voice chanted in its eternal phrasing.

"Hey, Sam, it's Sarah. I hope you had a safe trip back to Chicago. I was calling because I just got off the phone with Judith and she told me you were thinking of moving back here to Maine. I just thought I should call and tell you that I would like it very much if you did."

Suddenly, as though I was in college again, a smile broke through my empty expression. That was the final piece of assurance I needed, my decision was made.